EARLY IN ORCADIA

Naomi Mitchison

EARLY IN ORCADIA

British Cataloguing in Publication Data
A catalogue record for this book is available
from the British Library

ISBN 1 899863 50 8

First published 1987 by Richard Drew Publishing Ltd
This edition published by House of Lochar 2000

Printed in Great Britain by SRP Ltd, Exeter
for House of Lochar, Isle of Colonsay, Argyll PA61 7YR

This is how people's lives might have been a very long time ago, some five or six thousand years back. Yet, if we remember that we should count not more than three or four generations a century, there is no reason to suppose that men and women then were totally different from men and women now. Obviously they were puzzled and anxious about a number of things, some of which still make us puzzled and anxious. We solve one set of problems but others appear or are made. Remember what Robert Louis Stevenson said:

O, I wad like to ken — to the beggar-wife says I —
Gin death's as shüre to men as killin' is to kye,
Why God has filled the yearth sae fu' o' tasty things
to pree.
— It's gey an' easy speirin', says the beggar-wife to me.

The evidence of what these ancestors of ours were like is very slight. We don't know what they looked like. Nor do we know if any words of their language are still in ours or in any place names. But we do know that any individual then who left descendants who are alive now must be one of our own ancestors. Go far enough back and all humankind are cousins. I would like to think, for instance, that somewhere in my genes are the cave painters of Lascaux or the painters of the equally ancient Chinese or African caves and cliffs. To make it universal we must go back beyond the last ice age or we will cut off our cousinship with America and Australia. I can only hope that no human or protohuman genes have been totally lost.

Clearly people living in Scotland 6,000 years back are likely to be our ancestors, even if later waves of people succeeded them and probably killed many of them. We do know definitely that those of whom I write were farmers in the sense that they grew an early variety of barley and probably other things. They may even have planted or sown some kinds of plants with leaves or roots which could be eaten, perhaps near their houses. There are a great many edible plants which we don't bother about, or which have been improved so much over the centuries that they are really something else. We know about the animals that surrounded my people because bones survive and can be carbon dated. Pollen dating is more difficult.

So many of the activities of these ancestors left no evidence. Consider, for instance, weaving. There is no evidence which can be definitely counted on until we get to loom or spindle weights, and they were late. There are still people who fasten out the warp threads with wooden pegs and then get to work. The loom as we know it may be centuries, perhaps millenia, later.

Most of the evidence comes from tombs, which were more solidly built than houses and were also, perhaps, places which later generations would not meddle with. It is only rarely and because of some accident that actual dwelling houses survive, as at

Skara Brae. Most would be pulled to bits, the useful stones used for other houses, the roofing probably rotting off or used for fires. In the cultures where houses are built of mud and wattle in some form, the walls of one simply melt into the foundations of the next one. The old black houses in the Hebrides were used next for the beasts and then gradually fell down. Further east they turn into the great tels, or mounds.

One guess is as good as another about how people viewed the natural world. They did not build the vast time-measuring structures of the later people. Nothing tells us of gods or sacrifices. No doubt they puzzled about death when they had to. They must have been afraid and anxious, though not about some of the things which disturb us most. Certainly, the bones of some people at least were buried with care and probably with rites, but we can only guess and our guesses are structured by what seems appropriate to ourselves, many centuries, many religions beyond. We can only know that they must have been happy when Spring came, when the sunshine was warm and when they felt the touch of a loved body.

Stone and bone survive. We know the knives and axes. We know the animals associated with people. Today's archaeologists have cut down trees with sharpened stone axes, have cooked meat in stone troughs, ground grain, thrown spears and made hundreds of guesses. I join them in the guessing game, especially about boats. We do know that these people ate fish of species which are only found in deep water. That means they needed some kind of boat, some kind of fishing tackle. There is a puzzle, for instance, about deer. Their bones are found in early Orkney burials, but were they tame or wild? And how did they get to Orcadia? How? Why? When?

It is possible — I don't even say probable — that before my people, the first grain-growers, there were others already in some part at least of Orkney, hunters and gatherers, perhaps the people who brought in deer and seem to have managed the herds carefully. If so, they must have been very brave, remarkable seamen, not afraid of the open sea and, surely, adventurous. There is evidence of the settlements of such people all along the west coast of Scotland, from Kintyre to Lewis. Did they and the farmers meet and talk? Had they some words at least in common, surely sign and body language? We are singularly ignorant about pre-Aryan languages. I am almost sure that we, today, underestimate the intelligence, ingenuity and perhaps goodness, of our remote ancestors, who did not have to think, as we must, in terms of total world destruction, but who could concentrate on living.

The first time I saw that shining white line of Orkney I was with the Highland Panel in the late Forties. That stayed with me. It was almost a lifetime later that Marjorie Linklater took me to see the Eagle Tomb at Isbister. She knew it would wake something in me, as it did for John Hedges in his admirable book, *Tomb of the Eagles*. Looking down the long perspectives of time, I see alternatives. I have also bothered Colin Renfrew and R. L. Mercer, but they must not be held responsible for all the mistakes and misjudgments that are bound to have got into my story. I assume gaps of many generations between them, but there was continuity too, as I have tried to show. Who knows? Probably it wasn't like that at all. But yet perhaps it was.

Naomi Mitchison

There was an old man sitting close to the edge where
the grass was thin and many of the plants had thick,
salty leaves. He was the brother of the head man's
mother and many things were said about him, some of
them true. From the cliff he could see the whole of the
sea spread out below him full of streaks and changing
colours. Often it had things floating in it, twisted
about as though someone or something was pulling at
them. Sometimes all this moving and changing was far
down, but then — and he was beginning to know the
when — this whole sea reached up towards the old
man. Was it hungry? It ate the stones, but the dead
wood and branches stayed above, came and went. The
old man would look and say that this or that would be
carried away, visiting, but would come back at a certain time, and so it was. Equally the foam streaks and
the lines of colour changed but then returned. The
winds pulled them but also the moon. But how and
why? What fishing lines did the moon woman drop
into the sea?

The old man took these pictures of sea change into
his mind, though he did not any longer see the near
things clearly, not the small summer flowers, the

beetles and butterflies, his own bitten finger nails. The far sea was what he looked at. He had started this looking many summers ago, and he was now the oldest man. His children's children brought him food. 'What do you see, old man?' they would say. If there was honey he would lick it carefully while they waited and afterwards showed them, made them watch the sea, because some day something would happen.

How did he go on living? Somehow it was accepted that this had to been seen to. He had himself been a hunter in the days of his strength and now he had made a nest out of the skins of wild beasts whom he remembered killing. One of these was a bear. This bear had killed people, but he had not been afraid. He had killed that bear, himself. There was water in the heather pools. He went on watching. Sometimes others came and watched with him. It became known that he had the sea pattern behind his eyes. Perhaps one day it could be as plain as the land paths. All were careful to bring him food. Fish were split and laid in the sun until they smelled good. Sometimes a sheep or a calf was killed and a piece of the liver kept back for him. The same if a lucky spear or arrow found a deer or a wild pigling.

It was best to go up on a day of high sun. Then he would point to the patterns of the sea and beyond the sea the bright edging of something else, clear when the sun struck it, not always to be seen but certainly coming back. Perhaps a place. Perhaps with animals, with grass. Perhaps even with people. But not real people like themselves; that was not possible. People who were half animals, people as tall as trees. Sun people. Sometimes when things were going well, a few from the village would come and sit by the old man and tell stories about the shining edge, pictures they made up.

Someone would make a new, better story and then they all laughed and rolled about on the grass.

The most serious questioners were those who themselves went out on the sea and knew something about it and how it moved. But mostly they went, not onto the old man's sea but onto the other smaller sea which was between the bits of land which looked at one another and where there were other people. This was an easier sea. The boys rode on it when there were big bits of wood. But the grown men made real boats out of carefully bent hazel or ash branches, with skins sewn over them, boats big enough for three men. The skins could be pierced by properly pointed stones and then sewn with needles made from sharpened bones and sinews chewed and softened and rubbed between hands.

A specially good way of doing this might come about, but it was not always followed. Why not? You count the fingers and thumb. After one count you will have a name and you will help your mother in the field or your father with the sheep. Perhaps you are given a young dog. After two counts you may be given a spear and learn to make your arrows. You begin to like the smell of girls. Or if you are a girl you like to touch boys. At three counts you are a true man. But there are wicked beasts, wolves, bears, there are sea and rocks. There is also the making of babies pulling at your own life. Few lived beyond six counts and that was a pity because you had so little time to work out some new way of doing or being and show it to others.

In very good weather the men in the boats went further, fishing with lines for big, tasty fish. There was an island. It had a few sheep on it and, someone said, deer. There had even been people on it who must have brought the sheep, though the deer might perhaps have swum over. It was not a kind island; there were no trees for using or burning, only scrub willows and heather. The people were dead. Perhaps their fire had been put out by the rain and they could never light another. You cannot go on living if you can only eat small animals and seaweed and shells and there is no way of cooking. Perhaps they had been bad people. Nobody wanted to go on the island now, but there were fish to be caught easily round about it and in very good weather two or three of the boats were likely to go out there and come back with big catches. But the shining edge was far beyond it and the tearing streaky sea lay between.

The old man on the cliff had somehow not been killed by wild beasts, nor fallen off the rocks, nor died in the cold and wet weather. He had lived through a hand's count of wives who had kept him warm. His teeth had not fallen out. When he was a young man he was much in boats. He had thought how to lash his steering oar to the strong pole that went across the back of the boat. This had now become common. Certain ways of fishing were called after him. For you could catch fish in several ways, by hand or spear or with lines made out of the long hairs from sheep or cows tails or from the thinner hair on peoples' heads twisted together until they were strong. Mostly the boats were pushed with poles near the shore edge and if you saw a shell which was almost right for a fish hook, you would reach down and get it quickly. But also there were paddles of a kind if there happened to be a piece of wood that could be shaped a little with your hatchet stone.

But if the boat got beyond the easier water, out of the hands of the land, then it and the people in the boat might be caught and that was the end of them. It would happen once or twice in any lifetime; it would be talked about and then forgotten. The old man on the cliff knew about this, but somewhere inside himself he also knew that there was a something which would only come about because of being caught. That was a difficult thing to hold in the mind and often it slipped. But always it came back in the days of sun and growth and in the middle of the day when the sun was high and he and whoever was with him would see the shining, across the sea, across the danger. Surely there was something good, something wonderful. It was waiting. For those who would at last do carefully what he told them.

For it was coming clear to him and to some who from time to time watched with him and who had helped to break branches or find bits of fallen trees to carry down and launch and watch. Perhaps, yes, perhaps it would be possible for a boat to go with the same water that caught the branches and hurried them along. And this boat might even come back, having seen what was behind the Shining, for there were branches whose shape or markings they had stored in their minds and sometimes, perhaps after days, these came back. Mostly not.

After a time this came to be talked about, not only by the old men but by the young ones. They would meet between the houses. These houses were close, almost together. They were made partly out of the flat grey stones which could be lifted and put in place by a few working together and partly with turf and branches and skins. The head of the village, whose mother had been the old man's sister, had made a pattern on the flat stones at each side of his door. People like making patterns. It shows who you are. His was an important pattern. People stopped to look and run their fingers along the pattern, saying the names of the headman.

His house was near the biggest of the fires. He had two bed places and stone shelves, as well as a hollow stone for seething meat, which had once belonged to the sister of the old man. Also there was a place where part of the fire could be taken in, fed and then smoored during heavy rain. Even after a long and hard rain, the old ash of the big fire could be brought to life again if it had been properly covered; yet it was best for the headman always to keep a live fire in his house with the small smoke coming out between the patterns on his door. There was a story of a headman who did not do this because he was going to take his own daughter, so he was cut into small pieces and so was the girl and these small pieces were put together and there was a new fire. But perhaps this was a story of something that did not happen.

It was good to be near a fire and to smell cooking. But fires must be fed and they are greedy. They ate all the easy fallen wood. The women had to go far for more wood and they complained. There were bears and wolves, wild cats in the trees, wild boars in the marshes, foxes, stoats, snakes. The women shouted at the lazy men to come with them, to go ahead with spears and keep it safe for their mothers and sisters who were doing the hard work. One or two boys had to climb a tall tree and watch, and look for birds' nests while they were about it! Some of the women had stone hatchets; they could cut bushes and small trees and drag them out, then perhaps tie them with skin ropes for easier hauling. There was always plenty of yelling and screeching and then the long haul back, twice as hard if you had a baby on your back. But the men mostly gave a hand in this.

Everyone knew what kind of wood burnt best and which was sulky and smoked at you. Sometimes when you were looking for an easy bit to get at, you found a new place with berries and nuts; that was good. And again you might go, not into the woods, but along the shore. The sea often brought wood. And there might be things to eat sticking to it, cold, slatey things mostly, but not to be looked down on. The wood from the sea had to dry out, but once it was dry it burned with lovely sparkles; you could make stories out of it. So, one way or another, there was always enough wood for the fires. Luckily the fires could eat some kinds of heathery earth, but this must be dug and pulled and carried: work, work.

It was not only the women going into the woods who had to be guarded with spears or bow and arrows; the sheep and cattle must be guarded as well. If there were wolves about you did best to bring in the pigs and goats. Everyone needed to help as best they could. In the dark times hungry wolves would break through the thorn fences, and it was hard to feed the stock. Even without the wolves and bears you could not hope to keep your cows and sheep all alive over winter. At the beginning of winter people ate much meat, even the women. They felt strong. Then the babies came in the next summer.

Winter was hard enough for people. The women kept their grain in the big rough pots they had made in the sunny days. Any woman could make these pots, but only skilled women made the smaller, smoother pots. The women and their daughters ground down the grains from the prickly bere barley and made porridge or else flat slabs of bread, a little sour but filling you well and giving a comforting smell. Grain was the women's thing. Every house had a good, flat stone and another to pound and rub. Young girls would go down to the beaches to find their own stones. Most houses had a clay oven as well, standing on another flat stone. Sometimes the men begged or stole grain and made it come alive so that it sang in their heads. Even some of the older women did this with the men.

Further away from the sea there was another village, and again another and one beyond it. In summer they visited one another and found who could tell the most extraordinary and exciting stories. In one village they made good pots that were pleasing to look at and hold in the hand: they would exchange these for skins or good arrows or dried fish. Sometimes they quarrelled between villages, but not too badly; if someone was hurt there was a pretence that it had not happened. It was bad if people tried to hurt one another, very bad if someone was killed. People died because they fell or drowned or became too hungry or were clawed by beasts or were seized on by bad spirits. It was bad to make another person dead.

The boys and girls showed off to each other and sometimes a boy would carry off a girl into the thick wood and do what he wanted, or sometimes several girls would catch a boy and hold him and sit on him till he did what they wanted. After that they teased him with hazel switches and a kind of singing until he got up suddenly and grabbed one of them. All this was at the time when the sun only ran a little way under the edge of the world so that you could still see all night; but because things looked different in that below-roots light, people did things they would have felt shame doing in daylight when the sun could see them.

In each village there were houses made the same way. Sometimes the roofs were made with skins, sometimes with heather over branches, sometimes with things which the sea left on the beaches. It was known that these might be the bones of the giant fish that could be seen sometimes, a great black back heaving out of the water. In one village it was still spoken about, how one of them had been left on the beach after the sea had gone away and it had died and been eaten for many days until people began to become sick. But there the head man's house had a roof made from its bones.

That was a good story. Every village had stories. Also every village had what was not a house because it had no roof, only walls. Thick walls. This was for dead people. It was not good to look into it. Nor to smell it without making a special smoke. Someone who died was taken there quickly. Certain things might be done. But it was better not to think about it.

There were other villages further away. There was one across the small sea. Just sometimes and maybe after three or four summers, someone would come from one of them. It was mostly because of some trouble, but also there were those who brought gifts. Once a stranger had brought a kind of knife that was longer and stronger than other knives and tasted different on the tongue, just as this man's speaking was not sounding right. The knife did not come out of a stone. He was given a wife and became one of them and learnt to speak right, and threw away his stupid knife, but he was always afraid of the sea.

The sea raged at them in winter, shouting and screeching. It was in the so-dark winter that people made stories about the shining place at the far side of the sea which, even in winter, they could still see on a clear midday if they dared go up onto the windy cliff. Someone once said that over there you could find a place that was always summer, where there would always be green grass for the beasts and nuts and berries on the bushes. It was a good thing to make stories about. It made some people see it as real. Twice in the time of the old man's life it had made itself so real that people had set out in boats on purpose to go there. But that was the end. They were gone. Gone. As gone as if they had been put in the house for dead people.

The last to go had been one of the grandsons of the old man and another young man. Those two were tired of being among the last to eat when a sheep or a deer was killed. The older men, the strong ones who had the best spears and the best magic rhymes, they ate the best of the meat, the juicy, easily swallowed parts, leaving the bones and sinews for the young, who were fully as hungry. So these two had taken a skin boat which had been made by the uncle of one of them, and in it two lambs, the sheep-dog bitch belonging to one of them, which was due to pup, a young hind fawn that one of them had found, and a girl. They never came back. The sea got them, swallowed them like it swallowed stones. Not even giving back the bodies as it sometimes gave back branches, or as it gave back, but not always, the body of some child who had fallen out of a boat in a sudden wind.

It was bad, too, that they had lost that boat which had been made with so much care and skill, binding in cow-skins, already chewed into softness by many women, with strong sinews onto a framework of hazel. It had taken a whole summer of days and the breaking of several carefully made bone needles. Boats were difficult to build; they might seem fine on land, but once they were in the water they would tumble disobediently. Once or twice someone would see a big tree trunk floating and a picture would come into his mind of tree trunks tied together and floating, much stronger than the skin boats, the kind of big wood that the sea sometimes gave them. But how to do this? You could cut a small tree easily with a flint axe, but a big tree was difficult; it might try to kill you when it fell. And how to move it? How to get at it? The big old trees that fell by themselves were mostly rotten.

The old man on the cliff had sons and grandsons, and sons and grandsons from his sister. One of the older sons had watched a long time with the old man. It seemed to him that at certain times the thrown-in branches set towards the Shining, set as though with purpose. It also seemed to him that one or two of these — but could one be sure? — had come back. This man was more than five sets of fingers old, but he had kept his teeth and the skill of his hands. Most of that family seemed to live a little longer than most, even the women. This one was a son of the old man's wild days; he could not truly remember his mother, not to see, only to smell. The smell came back sometimes with his own wives.

He could have been the headman, but he did not like sitting and listening to quarrels or to being praised by those who were perhaps not friends. Nor was he interested in being the first to be served with killed and cooked meat. He had several names, but one of them just meant Hands, and that was how most of the village knew him. His early wives were dead, but he had a new wife who was called Metoo because of how she had been as a girl-child in a big family group: a survivor, that one. He had big children by his first wife; one of the sons had already got a house and a wife of his own. Also Hands had children by his second and third wives. Most could work, had value. The last two or three had died; the woman was getting too old for good milk. The eldest from his second wife was a girl-child who was clever with her hands and had come to know what leaves were best to eat after winter. She was friendly with Metoo and often ran behind her when the boys came sniffing after her. They called her Thinlegs after the birds that ran along the sand and were never near enough to be killed. She was known as a strong worker and soon enough it would be seen to that one of the village boys, perhaps a son of the headman, would get her as a wife. Maybe by the end of summer, in the eating time.

These two young women, Metoo and Thinlegs, watched what their man was doing; he did not say much, perhaps he could never get it clear enough, but they knew what was in his mind — the shining edge, and beyond it. Only one of his sons helped him; this was the third child from his first wife, a bit more than two hands old, not yet at full strength, a shouter and jumper. He was called Catcho because of a game he used to play. He had plenty of friends of his own age, but the boy he had been with most had been killed by a bear and that had made him sad and angry. This boy had come back several times into his sleep and wanted something. What? Catcho had never learned to swim, but both young women were used to swimming in the women's place a little way from the village where there was fine sand and sometimes weed drifting in which one could eat, or fat shells. In the sumer sun the water came over the sand and the women found they could float in the small waves as easily as the weed did and then that they could swim in it. Sometimes the seals came in and swam with them. The women and the seals sang together. Some of the men swam but not many, not the hunters.

Metoo had a baby in the fawn-skin slung on her back. She had even swum with the baby, which was another girl. She knew she would have a boy next. Easy. She was still suckling the baby girl, calling her Lovelove. But that was only her mother-name, not her real name. Hands looked at Metoo and touched her in a special way. She was the wife of his heart, she kept him young. There were five or six other children or half-grown boys and girls in the house from the earlier wives.

Now the long days were over. The women had gone out and gathered the heads of grain, the hard seeds of bere which had to be stripped of their prickles and pounded on a stone. Then came the storms. Sometimes they went on for days, the sea was totally an enemy. Blackness pressed down on them, clouds full of fear, swelling and closing in and bursting. The angry wind hurt people, threw them down if they stood straight. Hail prickled like wasps' stings. Gone the silver edge, perhaps it was broken off, would never come again. People huddled under piles of skins, not minding how clean they were, but the fur warmed them up; if they went outside they would pick up a goat or deer skin to wrap around themselves. The man of the house was warmest in the bed-place with a warm wife. The air in the houses smelled thick of people and sheepskins. Only the fires were kept up. The smell of cooked meat and sometimes bere bread was a good smell. It kept the night away and whatever crept through the night — wolf devils, six legged bears, dead people from the deads' house: ghosts. In the dark men and women moved about, groped at one another, pinched, bit, squealed. Fingers held on and moved about. The little clay or shell lamps were only small points of light and often there was no bird or seal oil. Sometimes there was singing, stones clicked together, sounds made from seeds or shells. Anything to make the dark lighter and keep the night things out. Metoo was good at stringing words to the beat of the clicked stones. More, more, Hands said, stroking her as she sang the words.

Hands had made her a pair of cow-skin shoes for the bad weather, when the snow bit at bare flesh. Before that she had only had skin strips tied over her feet in winter. If you had shoes with punched holes to thread a sinew through, it was better. You could pad them inside with grass or even sheep's wool, but they were difficult to hurry in, and Metoo liked doing things at a run.

In winter old people died because of the cold and dark. The old man was brought down from his perch on the cliff. They would have carried him, but he walked proudly and slowly and when he was down among the houses he complained that they were not well kept and the fires were smaller, which was not so, but everyone said yes, yes, it would be remedied. He sat down in the warm space between the head man's house and the fire and everyone rushed to bring him lamb skins with plenty of fur on them and to give him the drink made from grains that tingled warm in the throat.

It was in the dark months that children often died. They had fevers and pains in their chests. They coughed their small lives away. There was little milk for the small newly weaned but this was always half expected; it was the worst time for them; others would come out of the same mothers. You cried for a day, two or three days, but then it would be over. Hands lost one of his from the wife before Metoo: it had gone hot and there was redness on its body. Thinlegs and Metoo made a brew of leaves and roots to put on it, but there seemed to be no help. It was buried quickly beside the door, where it might feel safe; it had no name yet. Only those with names went to the house of the dead. If there had been a cure the women would ask one another what they had used: so a little knowledge was built up, but not enough.

During all the dark time Hands was making pictures inside himself and when the weather broke a little he went on with what he wanted to do. When there was a glimmer of sun he sat in the doorway striking flints; Metoo had to squeeze up to get past him when she had to go into the women's place. Sometimes Hands was so busy with his flints that he did it against a wall and Metoo shouted at him, or hit him with her cooking stick, but for all that they got on well enough and in a while Metoo began to tell her man what he must take in the skin boat. Hands listened and grunted. It was not real yet. But she was making it real. She began to sing it in a small voice. For him.

Spring came at last, more light, a little sun warmth. As soon as the sun had become strong enough to help them, some people began to take off the sheepskins which they had worn all winter, wool inside. They smoked them over fires to get rid of the biting crawlies. Then they put them back on. It was nice to be even a little clean. Some of them had bits of flat wood with teeth cut in them, or shells which they had broken cleverly with small stones so that they made a kind of comb which could help with cleaning the hair. That was nice too. But mostly they sat in the sun, picking one another over, popping the lice and nits and sometimes kissing between whiles. It was too early for breaking the ground and sowing.

There was a thing Metoo was doing for Hands while the baby lay beside her in a nest of soft skins. With her bone scraper sharpened she was going over and over the big cow hides for the boat, clearing off the fat but careful not to cut too deep. She made holes round the edges of the skins, which must be joined, and Hands knew about stuff to put over any small gaps where the water could crawl in and was carefully making it. But could it truly be going to happen? To go out onto this fierce sea that had shouted to them all winter so that you heard it even inside the houses?

But with the sun the silver Shining came back and this year, Hands said to himself, I will grip it. I can't have it there looking at me, me not knowing, not holding it. He began to wonder if perhaps it was truly a land. And if that was what it was, would there be people on it? And if that was how it was, could they be shining people, could they wear pure light instead of skin aprons and cloaks? Or would there also be shining lambs to clothe them? He dreamed of shining women and spoke of it to Metoo. She said that perhaps they were very big, as big as trees, stamping about, even the women. Could that be? Or perhaps they lived in holes in the ground. Why not? He began to talk about these people as though he had seen them. The two young women laughed together about that, though they always did their best to make him dream and talk about his dreams. Metoo strung necklaces of words about his dreams into patterns, songs, and that was good.

Already the headman had looked to see if the sun had moved round and was coming up from behind a certain rock. That meant that the digging sticks must be pulled out of their corners or new ones found and shaped. Work, work. People brought out their seed corn, smelled it, men and women together, trickled it through their fingers, compared it with their neighbours'. But Hands and Metoo were only going to plant half their seed. The other half — they looked at one another. Metoo laughed a little uncertainly. Hands caught and squeezed her up. 'Not here — there,' he said, and she gasped and coloured and nodded. It was all coming near, and could she bear it? But yes, yes.

The time came when the boat was almost finished, though the steering oar was yet to be lashed on. Hands carried it into the sea on a still day, helped by his son Catcho and two others. It was a big boat, bigger than any of the skin boats which had been made earlier. Other people's boats were either floating or still being mended and patched. Not such good boats as his. How would this big one lie on the water? They slid her in and let her lie. Yes, there were places where the water began to come through, but it was known that this could be patched over with moss and the stuff that came out of the pine trees. Hands had thought of that just as he had thought of the new thing for the bottom of the boat, a strong difficult long branch, in fact the top of a birch tree that had been split off in the storm. He worked on it for days with his hatchet, smoothing and shaping it. Hands was someone who looked at things and saw how they could do what he wanted. It had made the boat difficult to carry, just as it had been difficult and slow to sew over, but it seemed to make the boat steadier and stronger.

For a few days Hands pulled the boat about, learning its ways. He made a kind of heavy paddle, chipping away with his flint at a piece of fallen wood. Then he made another, a better one. At last he had made three. One day Metoo came down, baby and all, and got into the boat. Hands watched her for a while and then handed her a paddle. She was quick to see how to use it. At last he said in a soft voice, 'Good' and then, 'So you are coming,' and she answered in a straight way, 'To the Shining. Me and Lovelove.'

'The Shining' — he said it back. That was good, he had known she could say it, but he wanted it strong in his ears. The boat was balancing well and the wind was coming from the land — this was never a bad hard wind — and he thought to himself that two people could hold up a light skin on a frame of branches and the boat would go faster, even across the jumping waves. The thing behind his eyes had now become truer. There was still work on the boat, but there were other things to think about. When the lambs started to be born he chose a ram lamb and two ewe lambs. There was a bull calf and heifer calf. Could they try to take a fawn? A kid? Also there must be a firepot and small dry sticks to feed it. Metoo would see to that. But her grinding stone was too heavy; they would have to find one. If there was to be grain on the Shining. Metoo had kept back seed corn; she had it in a pouch of deer skin with a sinew tying it tight. But that must be planted and grow. It was difficult to think so far. The Shining is near, said Hands. He brought his fingers together showing how near. He and Metoo were lying together on a cowskin and she had taken Lovelove out of the sling and was now picking lice out of Hands' hair with a small stick, and the hairs themselves from his face and other places. All was nice-nice.

It now came to be known in the village that Hands, who was always respected, who was a man well known for all the things a man should do, was going to the Shining. They knew that he would get there, he said so, they said so. And then? Hands had much speaking with his half-brother, the headman, and often with the old man. By now the old man was back on the cliff, watching. They spoke to one another, looking at both the sky and the sea. The boat must be poled over quiet water so as to catch that long ripple. You see how the branches are running on it?

Who was to go in the skin boat? First there was Hands. Then there was Metoo and baby and Thinlegs. There was Catcho and two other young men, one of them almost three hands old. He had his eye on Thinlegs, but she shouted nastiness back at him. They tied the animals by their legs. They took flats of bere bread, but also the seed corn that Metoo had kept back for this. They took two fishlines and some hooks. They padded the bottom of the boat with sheepskins but they left a gap in the deepest part. Hands knew that bits of waves were bound to break in even on a good day, and he had two of the big shells with crinkled backs but inside like a part-bent hand, to scoop the water back into the sea. The boat was steady in the water with more weight in it, but also the little waves came higher up on the side. You had to think, oh to think so hard, to make pictures in your mind of what might happen and what you could stop happening. They had meant to take a skinful of fresh water but that sunk the boat too much, so at last they only took what would go into a sheep's bladder, although that had a bad taste. Surely there must be water on the Shining! Hands took his spears, he and the young men all took bows and arrows. Catcho had a light spear, the best kind for fish.

When he got back from the hill and from talking with the old man, Hands had a clear picture in his mind of how he was to go the way of the branches which had been thrown in. He had even began to call his boat The Branch. So what else? The young children could go on living in his house. Two of them knew about sheep and would care for the bere that was coming up well. The others, one of whom had no name yet, would learn. The rest of the village would see that they took their turn on wood-gathering and were given their turn when there was meat. Perhaps one day — but no, you could not hold two things in your mind, going and coming back.

The old man came down from the cliff to look at the boat. He told Hands some strings of good words which would help the boat to find and keep to the long streak of water which might take them past the island and on to the Shining. What mattered now was to be sure that the moon was a certain size and rose in a certain place so that the water would be pulled, just as women were pulled by the moon, their mother. It would be best, said the old man, to paddle the boat out of their own quiet water and as near as could be to where the big pulling-ins began. It should be carried towards there before it was floated. Hands could almost have carried the boat empty but certainly not with all the things that they were taking. So everything was taken out and carried. Most of the village came to help while Hands and Catcho and the other boys got the wet boat onto their shoulders and started off along the shore, treading carefully in the path that wound through the rocks and whin bushes, just above high tide mark, among sea pinks and campions and primroses, and bits of dry seaweed blown onto the land. Everyone knew just how to place each foot going round and over the hard jags. But in a new place? No, that could not be held in the mind's sights.

It was all very exciting. People sang or shouted good words, carried the young beasts through flowers. The young men laughed a lot but not easily. Metoo and Thinlegs got hard jokes from the boys which they had to toss back. The baby slept through it, warm in its fawn-skin sling. There was the good little cloud in the sky which meant that the wind was asleep.

And then, they were in the boat. As they had been planning, but it was real now. The boat called Branch. And it moved, it took them away, away from everything. It seemed low in the water. But the old man was sending words after it and watching. He could see the boat well although he could not always see clearly what he was eating. He could see that first they were poling and paddling, going slowly, and then the old man saw that they were holding up the framework of skins and he took a great gulp of air and clenched his fists. And quickly, quickly, the boat and the little people in it had gone beyond the headland and the sea seized on the boat Branch as it had seized on little branches and sticks.

How had it taken so short a time? When they came to the first edge of the sea, the white fierce ripple, it had caught Branch, swung her around and the water had leapt in, cold and angry. Metoo and Catcho had scooped it out as hard as they could, not speaking, just working. But Hands had shouted the words that the old man had told him while he pushed onto the steering oar with all his weight and the boat had heard the words, had obeyed him, had turned, had caught the smell of the Shining and while they were still bailing and Branch had rocked and jumped like a woman under a man, they were going fast on a piece of water that was somehow a different colour and the Shining began to come near.

And yet it was no more the Shining, it was black rocks, glaring at them. It was going to eat them and the sea was hurrying them into its mouth. How to escape? Afterwards Hands could never remember clearly. Only the oar burrowing into his chest and could he hold it and if it broke or the thongs snapped —— ! For a moment he caught Metoo looking at him and she gave him strength, she knew he could do it. Because of Lovelove. But they were near, near. He could see, could smell the crowd and clamour of birds on the black rocks and the sea pulling at Branch. And then suddenly the sea had let go, was taking them another way and Branch tumbled and spun. Catcho and his friends had the poles out, not that they could have saved Branch if the rock had determined to eat them. But Branch was whipped about by new waves which drenched and blinded them, and suddenly the black rocks swung back and there seemed to be an opening if they could get there. Not this one, round again. Hands shouted to the boys to paddle, hung onto the steering oar, spray in his face. And somehow they were off the black teeth of the rock and into water which he could trust. But what had happened? There was one less in the boat, one of the boys had fallen in and the rocks had eaten him. Perhaps that was why they had let the rest go. Him and the others.

If that one had been a woman Metoo thought, he might have swum, not sunk like a stone. He must have been poling them off, standing. But even if he had swum, the rocks would have got him all the same. The rocks, the rocks, going high, high into the sky and where was all the Shining? Oh how wet, how cold they were, oh poor Lovelove! But now they had been swept into quieter water and beyond was the look of somewhere they could walk on. Grass? Yes, it was green, with sunlight patching it bright and friendly. It was like their own. Trees. Now they had come between bits of land and there was a choice to be made.

Away from the rocks, keep away, that was in Hands' mind strongly. And it was the way the sea was taking them, rocking them along. Catcho was crying for his friend. He had tried to hold his arm and almost fallen over himself, but the hungry sea had eaten his friend. But had the other one called — the friend who had been slashed by the bear, broken and bitten — who wanted — company? Catcho was suddenly very frightened, right inside himself. He yelled to the rocks to keep away, not snatch at him!

But Hands shouted: 'Try the poles' and Catcho was jerked out of it. Both of them picked up the poles and began to feel with them while Thinlegs took the paddle. The dead were left behind. And at last they felt bottom and it seemed that the Shining accepted them. The lambs and calves lifted their wet heads and complained, yet perhaps they too felt the land near.

There was a reach of sand, they could see it under the boat when the sun shone, bubbling, living. Was this then truly the Shining? The sea pulled them in but then pushed them back. They could smell land. Hands shouted to the young men and they screamed back at him, pains in their hands and backs and minds, two where there should be three. Suddenly Thinlegs jumped into the water and began to swim, catching and pushing the back of the boat when the waves tried to pull it away. And then slowly they were coming nearer the land. The poles were getting a grip, held, and Branch was going nearer, nearer, and Thinlegs touched bottom and got a better purchase against the heave of small waves. And now Catcho jumped out to join her and they were only knee deep. 'Out, out!' Hands shouted at them, not wanting any damage to the bottom of Branch, for there were small rocks here that could tear the stretched skins. Everything must be got out. Careful with the fire pot. There, take it, Metoo! Up, up.

The young beasts were untied. Only a few breaths and they were on their feet, staggering a little, shaking themselves and then quickly beginning to nibble away at the young grass. Metoo walked straight up to the top of the small ridge and looked over. Grass and the same plants and flowers she knew, the same leaves and roots to be eaten or not to be eaten. Creeping willows, berries, bigger bushes and trees beyond. In among them fallen wood, easily gathered. She felt round and picked the baby out of the fawn skins that had kept her dry and warm, 'Look, Lovelove, this is the Shining!'

In a hollow, sunwarmed, she and Thinlegs made a fire. Smoke went up. They brought down sticks. All that had been in Branch now came into the hollow. They ate a whole round of the bread, almost the last they would get for a long time. Metoo was already thinking of digging sticks so that the new plot of seed corn could go in quickly before it was too late. It would have to ripen, yes, Metoo thought, we must make it ripen, we must all tell it and then it will hurry and then we shall pick the ears and there'll be more for next year. More, more. Perhaps more everything, more birds' eggs, more sea-shells, more fish, more berries, more things to eat. But we must build a house.

The two big boys were down by the edge looking for shells to eat or to use for bait, but they were sad, sad. If only —— But they would never see him again. They had to forget. They had helped Hands to carry the empty boat up over the ridge. 'Our house,' said Metoo. At least it was shelter. Hands went into the wood to find brushwood to go at the back of the boat so that Branch could rest comfortably and allow them to use her as part of a house. He tugged and pulled and the brushwood followed him. The wet sheep skins were taken out and put in the sun, but it would be a while before they were dry. Meanwhile, all of them started dragging at the brushwood and fallen branches. Yes, here was a piece that would make a digging stick. All that was needed was a few strokes from Hands' stone hatchet. Good.

Hands went further into the wood quietly, carrying his spear. It was a scrappy wood, no big trees but a tangle of small ones and thick bushes. But no bears, no wolves, no wild cats, no wild dogs, no smell of them anywhere, no footprints. Or could that be a sheep's hoofmark? An old mark? Hardly. Perhaps? But he dug out a nest of mice, good eating, burn off the fur, spear them on sticks and they were ready. Just the same, you could catch a bird easily; they hardly moved away. The fire grew bigger from the wood they brought in. The smoke went up. There was a wet place in the wood. Metoo scooped a hole in the earth. Yes, it was good water. She filled the bailing shells and a small pot which would go on the fire. Thinlegs found a plant she knew that had nutty roots and was easy to pull up. It was all good. But where had the Shining gone? Where was what they had been looking for?

All slept between the Branch upturned on her side

and the fire. Morning came and the fire must be fed. Metoo, half asleep, snuggling against Hands, gave Thinlegs a kick to wake her for the fire. And as Thinlegs rolled over and woke grumbling, she saw something at the far side of the hollow. A head. The head of a person. Thinlegs dropped back again, pretending to sleep, but watching from half-shut eyes. Slowly the head came nearer on shoulders, crawling. And another by it.

But they were persons. Truly persons. They were not the Shining people that Metoo and Hands had made stories about. They were not different. In a while there seemed to be three of them. But when Thinlegs at last moved, the heads bobbed down, vanished. She touched Metoo and whispered, and so the whisper went round. Hands got to his feet and stretched. He had been deep asleep and in his sleep there had been voices and faces. But they were good. He shook his head when Thinlegs wanted to wake the boys. 'I will see,' said Hands, and went by himself to the top of the ridge. Yes, he could see the persons at the edge of the wood; he called gently. Yes, they were real persons. The big one was a woman and Hands suddenly found it in his mind that a new woman might be good, might be a gift for him from the Shining. He moved towards them and saw that the others were young, a girl perhaps ten fingers old or a little more, and a boy not full grown. They had no furs on them, nothing to keep the wind away, and they were thin — you could see their bones — but the woman seemed to have the remains of a skin apron and necklaces made of grasses and pieces of shell. Hands went near and said 'Who are you?' Then the woman laughed and pointed to the sea and said 'You come from there?' He thought she was partly frightened, partly happy. She came near. Then all at once she came very near and touched him on the place that men have and that knows how to answer. She had a strong smell, but that did not matter. From a little way off the children looked on but they did not know what their mother was doing and why she made sounds as though she was eating a roast fish after hungry days.

Thinlegs too had looked on from behind the ridge, but she did not tell Metoo. She had found some leaves which softened nicely in the heated water. And the roast mice! There were shells enough for everyone, good, good. When the boys woke there were three new people, though the young ones were scared and would not come near. So the woman began to tell her story and they all called her the Shining even though she was far from that. She spoke in jerks as the words came back to her. It seemed that when those two young men had set out a long time ago in a small boat, oh so much smaller than Branch, they had carried her along, not very willing but they were rough boys. And then the boat had been carried past the black rocks and into this place, where the sea was quiet. But it had broken on the rocks a little further on. They had brought a fire pot with them, 'Yes' said the woman, 'the same as that one. Your fire pot. I carried it. I did. We lived here for very many years. They became strong men, hunters, but one of them was drowned — and I had children but some died and the other man died so now there are three only; the three you see.'

'How did you eat?' Hands asked.

'Things from the sea. Birds' eggs. Sometimes small birds. The men hunted. Seals. Big birds. Lizards. The dogs helped. I have fire,' she said proudly, 'and I have kept it alive.' And then: 'So long a time.' She was beginning to speak more clearly.

'Are there wolves?' Hands asked. 'Bears, deer, lynxes, anything?'

She shook her head. 'Sheep only.'

They looked at one another and wondered 'From your boat?'

She nodded. 'The lambs of our lambs. Many sheep now. But it is hard to get them. A stone must be very lucky to get one on the head.'

'We can do better,' said Catcho, and he was thinking that the girl who wore no clothes and was a little ugly, the young one, would grow soon, for she was half woman shaped, and then she would belong to him, Catcho's woman. He would kill a sheep with his bow and arrow and give her an apron made out of a skin so that her woman shape could grow and this thought covered his sadness at the drowning of his friend.

'My dogs' said the woman. 'They catch fish for me. Sometimes rats.' Had there been a dog in the boat? Long, long ago, how could one remember? Rats? Yes, that was the old word that the old people used; the young people had a new, scuffling word now. Hands thought back. Yes, there had been a bitch on that boat long ago.

'You are here,' said Hands slowly, chewing it, 'all the years you were dead. Taken by the sea.' He shook his head. 'You were eating. All those days. You were a woman of us. Not of the Shining.'

But she shook her head, puzzled, only half understanding, for the words were not quite her words. She did not know this word, the Shining, that he used. She was the same; he was the different one. Later perhaps she would understand. But now she felt calmed inside herself; it had been a real man, not some ghost. She had seen many ghosts at first, a long time ago. This man might have been a ghost, but no, he was real. She could feel him still. Perhaps he would have food. She called softly to the children who had run away.

And so it was — and what food. She had forgotten. Metoo broke pieces off the last of the flats of bread, warm and chewable from the water, but not big pieces for there would be no more for a long, long time, after the winter which was bound to come, after the melting of days. The woman put the piece in her mouth, remembering, turning it round and round with her tongue. But the young ones had not seen bread, not ever. They drew back. How thin, how sad, thought Metoo, and gave them instead a big handful of shells, something they knew. They grabbed the shells and ate quickly, looking round, not able to believe, not yet.

Metoo was sad for this woman who was so alone. Perhaps she had forgotten her name, perhaps she had no name. It had gone, it was a ghost. So Metoo called her by the sister-name. Hands was glad of that. But he had to be clear on what mattered. 'Now tell,' he said to the woman. 'I looked. Saw no tracks. Tell me: bears, wolves, what bad beasts?' He had to be sure.

She shook her head, repeated, 'Only rats, mice. Small beasts. Many birds. We get eggs, eggs, eggs. Young birds. And then none. Not in the bad time, the cold. Only what the sea gives.'

'So you are hungry most days?'

She looked away. It was true. The two that died because she had no more milk for them. The other, older. Ghosts now, hungry ghosts. Angry at her. She began to cry, without moving; she had become afraid. Big tears ran down her face. There was food here, but was she in? Could she and her children be part? Then Metoo took her hand and stroked it and said 'You have a house?' The woman nodded uncertainly and

Metoo went on: 'You have a nice house? A good house? Show me?'

The woman stopped crying and took Metoo's hand and then peered at the baby Lovelove, so warm in lamb's wool and fawn skins, and smiled. Better than ghosts. Oh yes, yes. The girl child cried out because Catcho had fingered her, but she was clumsy with words. Hands spoke sharply to the boy. Later, it might be. 'We will see your house,' he said. They walked over the rise in the ground. Suddenly he smelled sheep; beyond the next rise he saw them. Thin sheep, not like his two lambs would be. 'If we can catch one,' the woman said hesitantly, 'we get a little milk. Sometimes. So little.'

'When my heifer calf grows you will see good milk,' said Hands, and wished that he had after all brought piglets. If there had been higher sides to Branch. Next time. Next time. It was all coming clear to him. He would live long like the Old Man, he would trample on the waters!

A thin dog came rushing at him and Metoo, but the woman called to it sharply and it dropped, growling. In a hollow there was a kind of house, turf piled into low walls, weeks of work with a digging stick. The roof was low, branches from one of the low twisted birch trees covered with a bad-smelling sheep skin. Perhaps, Hands thought, it had been pulled and cut off a dead sheep never properly cleaned, what could a lone woman do? In front of the house there were stones round a small fire pit, a few little clay pinch-pots, empty, and a pile of old shells and fish bones. Sad, sad.

'We will build you a better house,' said Metoo. 'See, Sister, we are many persons now.' She patted the woman on the arm. She would be able to show her the big grain pot, her own beads, everything. She would be Big Sister to this one.

'And your boat?' whispered the woman.

'One day,' said Hands, 'Branch will go back. Not yet. But I have done it. I am here. Oh, what I will tell!' The two women watched him while he thought proudly of how he would tell everyone about the Shining, and he danced a little with his feet like a young boy might dance. It was getting late in the day. The sun had come round to look at them and was beginning to drop. There was another grass ridge with some heavy rocks on it, too heavy for one woman, but two men, perhaps three men, might be able to move them to make the beginning of a strong, good house. Hands climbed up and over and there was the sea suddenly again, and the streaky water ways and there beyond, was another Shining. As he looked it came to him that this was the Shining he had come from. Yes, that must be so. But he could not altogether get it into his mind that there were two Shinings. If you saw yourself in a still pool there were two faces: was it somehow the same? But had he been there, behind this Shining he now saw? And had those dead men whom he now remembered a little, those fool boys who had stolen the boat and the girl, who had been taken by the sea — but yet had stood here, on this ground, alive — had they seen this Shining? He looked in his mind. He must kill those old things he had half thought and made into stories. So that the two Shinings could face one another and he would know them both. Yes, that was it.

The boys would have liked to explore and build a house, but Metoo shouted at them and made them get digging sticks and help her and Thinlegs get in the seed corn, breaking the hard top of the ground with their digging sticks, pulling up the grass and weeds from round the holes, putting two grains in each. Both the women spoke good words over the buried seed so as to make it live in the womb of the earth. And it must hurry, hurry, its friends back at home were already showing their first fingers. But perhaps on this new ground, facing the sun, so much wanted, loved, they would come quickly. They must! By now Lovelove was crawling everywhere, grabbing at anything, wouldn't stay still. The sister woman had offered to help with the corn, but she had forgotten the words and if they were said wrong it would be bad. So she helped with other things, most of all a fence of stakes and prickles round the corn patch. Her own two children kept close to her, while Hands was off, looking for the right site for their new house. He turned things over in his mind: should he let Branch be his roof? But no, no, Branch was precious, must have a house of its own, well sheltered, because — because ——

Hands looked about. He was not going near the hollow where the sister woman had made her sad house and where, no doubt, her other children were buried: the place where she, a named person, had been alone, except for the children, while years passed, long, long. Soon she would whisper her name. Good to have two women, thought Hands, but she must stay in her house. Her smell would be wrong in his own house. In his there would be the bed-place for Metoo, the softness, the knowing what his mind said to him, even before he knew it himself. And Lovelove. He did not remember the other babies. Not even Catcho, his best boy. He had been frightened, went off on a long hunt, but his wife then, the one with the mark on her cheek, screamed and screamed. But he had brought back meat, they had killed a big he-pig. His spear. He had given her as much pig meat as she could eat while the new baby squirmed beside her. He did not like to look at it. He had hollowed out the pig's tusk and ground down the edge and point. Later it had broken. If he thought hard he could still see the tusk. But not baby Catcho. And his next wife —— But here, surely, was the place for their house, only a few good flat stones to be seen, but plenty of others. Wind shelter and the small, friendly, bubbling stream. You would hear it at night.

When Hands came back to tell them about his house place, the planting was done and the boys down by the sea getting shells. Metoo was standing on a rock with deep water on two sides and the fish line baited with a limpet she had knocked off with her stone. Thinlegs had Lovelove on her back and was looking through the plants that crawled among the stones, nibbling or putting them into her rush bag. Hands watched as Metoo landed a fish, liking to see her arms and neck in the sunlight, her strong legs, her clever fingers, the dangle of still milky brown-nippled breasts. In his mind he could feel the round softness of her. As she jumped down he caught her and the cold wet fish wriggled between them till they were both laughing and laughing. He pulled her in behind another rock, flipping her apron away. Yes, this was it, the Shining he wanted.

It was hard work, making the new house, fitting in the stones, chopping at wood, tearing at turf. It must be big enough for them all, with a bed place for him, big enough for the man who had crossed the sea and found the Shining, and for Metoo in beside him and the whispering stories they told one another, with thick bedding of dry bracken and the warm sheep skins spread over and under them. He planned it, she laughed, it happened. By now the young beasts had been put in a green patch near the little stream with a fence of light boughs twisted in and out between stronger stakes. 'You get me a ewe with two lambs,' she said, 'we will kill one, eat him, then there will be milk for Lovelove.'

'Why? You have it,' said Hands, running his fingers down over her nipple so that they became damp with sweet-tasting milk.

'Maybe not long,' said Metoo, 'get you a boy. But you get a ewe. Get two ewes. I want.'

The next day Hands, the boys, Thinlegs and Sister's two children all went off after the ewes, which seemed to be in two or three small flocks. If the dogs had been trained they could have helped, but Sister's dogs were only trained to get fish. It could be she had no knife sharp enough to kill a sheep. A woman could not make an old knife come alive again as a man could. Not any man. But himself, Hands. They cornered two ewes, one with a pair of lambs, knocked them on the head till they were stupid, brought them back and put them in the green patch. Metoo and Sister had got some still stronger stakes for the fence. Metoo was clever with a hatchet but poor Sister had only the broken head of one. No wonder things had gone badly for her. When the ewes woke up and stood, Hands held their horns, Catcho their back legs, and Metoo milked them both a little. They must get used to it. Later they killed and roasted one of the lambs. How Sister enjoyed it! Metoo dipped her finger in the ewes milk for Lovelove and then gave her a small dab of marrow from one of the bones. The lamb skin was pegged out, it would make an apron for Sister's girl, her first, but she must be the one to keep on scraping and chewing it soft.

Other things had to be done while the good weather lasted. Sister showed them a wet place where there was slimy clay that could be dug out, pounded and squeezed, then made into small pots and dried in the sun. But these always broke away into powder. Not good. Later perhaps they would dig a fire hole and make good pots, real ones. She had brought one porridge pot, but she was wondering if it would stand in the ashes; there was a small crack. Metoo thought Sister might have made a fire hole, and asked her. Sister said she had tried once, when the men were still there to help make a fire pit, but it went wrong, the pots broke and she did not try again. She had never learned. 'Where did you do it?' Metoo asked.

The woman pointed. 'There. Where the wood stops. We had a house. A good house. But he — he became ill and then dead. I left him in the house.'

'Did you put stones?' Metoo asked in a hard voice, and Sister went down on her knees.

'Yes, yes,' she said, 'big stones. Heavy. I carried them and I was hungry and the little thing I had last, it was dead too. So I put her in with him so they are both — both of them — they cannot hurt! Big stones.'

'Show me.'

But Sister shook her head. 'No, no, I made my other house. You saw. Sometimes they come out but not — not like People. No.'

'You see them?' Metoo asked, but Sister only shook and cried. Metoo was sorry for her and thought no wonder her pots broke.

When they had finished their house, Hands got Branch back into the water and they poled her cautiously along the shore line until there was a break and they could see far, far, nothing but sea. No Shining. And Hands felt uneasy. There was more land beginning past the break, but the big sea pushed waves at Branch. It was best to go back. They had dropped lines into the edge of this other sea where there were streaks and bubbles and had caught some big fish, a new kind. Most were caught by Catcho's friend, who was the best at fishing, so much that they called him Fishfish. But Catcho still dreamed of his other friend and in his dream he caught him before he fell into the sea. How could it not come real? But it never did.

Fishfish was more careful. So as to be safe Hands threw one of these new fish to the seals of which there were many, thanking them for their company. They were the brothers of the seals they had known in the old days. Poling back, with the bright fish flapping at the bottom of Branch, they found there was one small place along a seam that let in wetness, but there was moss and Hands still had some of the pine tree blood which he smeared into it. Now Branch could rest again.

That was an evening when Hands walked about, thinking, while Metoo was cleaning and cooking the fish and talking to Catcho. Hands came on Sister who lay down at once and got what she wanted, not a ghost. Hands enjoyed it, though not as much as he would have liked because she had a less nice smell than Metoo. She was altogether less nice. Perhaps she knew but he did not say. It could just as well have been something for Catcho or even Fishfish but they were not much interested. Once or twice they had teased and fingered the girl, and it seemed to Metoo that if the girl went on eating well, she could be ready in another year or so to be a wife for them. That would be good. Already the girl was picking up words and laughing a little. She was keen to learn and Metoo liked teaching her how to trim and chew the lamb skin, how to weed round the little seedlings as they came up, how to take the rough bits off roots with a good stone scraper. The boys called her Barebum at first and the name stuck.

There were things which still had to be found, most of all two stones, one with a hollow so that you could stand it by the fire, put in pieces of meat and then, using two green sticks, drop in the hot stones out of the heart of the ashes, so that the water would heat and steam and the meat would soften. You lost too much, roasting over the fire and the good fat dripping out, but somehow people liked their meat cooked; it was easier on the stomach. Also it showed that people were not wolves. The other stone was of course for the grain which must be shaken out of its prickly head and then made to lie down and be beaten. Metoo searched along the beaches and marked to herself those she thought might be good stones, but heavy. Hands and the boys would have to see which could be lifted. She saw that there was plenty of seaweed where the sea had left it, good to chew, good for the beasts to nibble.

Then she went to look at the corn shoots, coming on well, but they must hurry, hurry, to be in time for the ripening. She knocked on the soil and made a pattern with her fingers and whispered; then she laid her ear down. Yes, she heard something which could be an answer. She was glad she had seen this being done, just once when she was a child, once more when she was growing, but she remembered. The exact sharp pointed words. Oh yes, Metoo remembered.

There were bramble bushes growing here and there in the edges of the wood. She ate as many as she could and stuffed a few into the rush bag which she always carried, along with trails of seaweed and a few shells, their middles easily picked out with a sharp twig, salty and nice. There were bits of wool from the sheep catching on the brambles. She picked off bits and stuffed them in as well. A few bramble berries squashed and she painted her arms with them. Now she could look across at the Shining which, she now understood, was where she had come from. Often she and her friends had painted themselves with bramble juice when there were so many berries. Over there.

And the wool? She stuck her fingers into it among the strong sheep smells. It would make into a fishing line or a necklace or to wash oneself; it was soft, soft. She slipped the sling off her back and put Lovelove down to crawl in the grass, gave her the juice of a squashed berry. There were flowers that tasted nice when you chewed them up, honey flowers.

She had quite a lot of wool in the bag, two big handfuls; sitting beside Lovelove she twisted out a small grey-brown cord, then another and still another, almost the length of her arm, stretching the wool out from the bundle. They looked nice on the grass. Playing with them, she began to put them across one another, in and out like a sheep fence. Lovelove tried to grab, but Metoo turned her round and herself moved away a little to play with her fence. A sheep fence made of wool! She patted it. A mouse could hide underneath. And suddenly she had an idea. She began to pull longer and longer twists of wool out of the mass and laid them in and out. She pushed Lovelove away, at last bundled her back into the sling. The baby started screaming, but it didn't matter, not now, not when Metoo had the picture in her head of what she wanted to do.

There, she had criss-crossed the wool into — what? She laid it carefully on a stone and admired it. Then she picked up screaming Lovelove and stopped her mouth with a dripping nipple. The baby gulped and choked and yelled again, but Metoo held her close and rocked her, singing words to her, words strung in and out. But how to keep it, how to stop the ends coming loose? With a rush basket you plaited the ends in and out, but the wool wouldn't stick. Or would it? If you tied the ends over something. If you knotted them. But longer pieces. Suddenly she didn't like the smell of sheep in the wool. She threw it away. Lovelove went to sleep. She picked the wool thing up again. She was going to take it out and look at it, perhaps often, in her mind.

Winter, when it came, could have been worse. They knew it might be bad, but at the end they were all living. It had been sore on them, not having the other people, the knowledge of houses and warmth somewhere near, keeping out the long nights and the wild beasts. It was hard to believe that there were truly no bears or wolves prowling. Sometimes the wind howled like wolves. They talked about wolves, but already wolves were becoming a story.

They would count over the good things, the warm skins, the meat smoked over the fire and hung from the roof, the roof itself, strong birch branches covered with turf. The pot of seed corn. Only half the ears had ripened and set. Metoo had kept back almost all, had only allowed them one pot of porridge as a feast for everyone. But even that was not proper porridge because she had no big flat stone for grinding — not yet — and could only bash the grain roughly. Next year, yes, next year, she would have a good grindstone and then an oven if only she could get the right clay for it. Plans, plans! Meanwhile there was only one crock to stand in the ashes and heat up; it had to do for soup or porridge. Only she and Thinlegs could touch it, not the boys.

There had been some half ripe ears left after the good ones had been taken. These unripe ones were good to chew when you had pulled off the prickles. Sister's small boy had stolen some and been beaten; he must learn. Those two young ones and Sister still liked to live in their own house, although they came over sometimes, mostly when they smelled food. There was great eating for a while after Hands speared the big seal. Sister told Metoo that once she had been called White Bird. But that was no name for her now, and she knew it.

After the last of the heads had been cut off the sheep were allowed into the fenced corn patch. They gobbled up the stalks and the weeds. When the waves left a big present of brown sea tangle, all of them picked up armfuls and threw them to the sheep. This was how people had always done it. Always. People with sheep and corn. This was how it had been at home. It seemed that what came out of the sheep went into the corn. But the brushwood fence was getting patchy. The sheep could break through. Metoo went walking among the sheep, telling them to eat and shit, saying the right words which she had heard her mother saying and kept in her head.

In the dark time Metoo and Hands stayed long in the bed place. Thinlegs put more wood on the fire, took what little milk there was from a ewe that still had it, made soup from whatever was brought in. There was the one good crock that could stand in the ashes. But careful! Careful! Metoo made more rush baskets for storing. They never lasted long and some things slipped through them, would be better stored in pots if there were enough. Next year she would try to make some more. And one to keep as the porridge pot. For next year's corn! Thinlegs watched the birds and squirrels hiding their nuts, then she robbed them. There were not as many good nut bushes as there had been in the old days in the old woods. Perhaps if one planted branches they might turn into real nut bushes; she might try.

Catcho found hedgehogs, good eating, these, One could crack and suck every bone. How had they come across to the Shining? Perhaps floating on some bit of wood. For there were always bits and pieces; the most they had found were in a corner of one of the small bays, presents from the big sea, for them. Twice they had seen deer, but Hands had said to let them be until there were more; these few must have come from the fawn which had been brought in the boat long ago. They were small. It would be best to get another if — when —— There were always shells; some were specially good and juicy. Lovelove squatted on the ground and played with them, talking to them, or else climbed into the bed place with Metoo and Hands.

Metoo felt herself swelling. Hands ran his fingers over her. 'See what I have done,' he said. 'Me too, me too!' she whispered back and they both laughed. She became altogether rounder. His fingers loved to trace the roundness all over her, the smoothness that delighted the palms of his hands. Once on a sunny day they went down to a small sheltered beach of fine sand and Hands made a sand woman with beautiful upcurving belly and thighs, wide hips, marks in the sand where the woman place could be. Metoo looked at it and thought this is a me he has made. But the sand blew and shifted and he turned back to Metoo, to the real flesh, to warmth and touch.

On a bad day in the cold time, the long nights, it was best to stay warm, never to get out of the bed-place till it was time and weather for a hunt. But Catcho would be off and out, trying for some beast and sometimes counting over the sheep on his fingers. Once one of them fell over a steep place and he and Fishfish managed to get it back, limping a little; but it would live. There was enough grass for them, but he had cut some while it was still good and let it dry in the sun and wind; then he took it into the house and slept on it himself. This was for the two calves which were growing big and strong, but too thin. He had even made them a kind of shelter.

The darkest time was beginning to give way to the sun, and one day Catcho brought back Barebum, Sister's girl, to come and eat with them. She was laughing and bleeding a little and it was clear to the rest what had happened. But Metoo thought it was too soon. Barebum would soon start looking like a real she-person; he should have waited. 'We must feed her,' said Metoo and made her drink a kind of soup from the seal meat and some shore plant, which the girl did not like much. But Catcho held her while Metoo tipped it into her mouth and when she sputtered he put his hand between her legs. After that she often came to the house and took her share of whatever was cooking, and began to laugh with the others and learn to sing. Now she was talking like a person, but she could not join the talk of what went on in the other Shining.

And now the dark time was shortening. There were tufts of young green grass and the beasts were at them all the time. The sheep began to stray and Catcho was teaching one of the puppies to help him, as the dogs used to do on the other side. Hands began to prowl all over the island. Now he was beginning to understand that there was more land beyond the gap where the big waves came rolling in. But it was never a Shining. It lay like a humped blanket over the line of the sea. So what could be there? What would he find there?

One day Metoo felt something happening inside her. She knew what it would be. It would hurt but it was exciting, this happening. She called to Thinlegs and they went down between the rocks. If she cried out the noise of the waves hid it. She twisted round, got on all fours like a beast, felt squeezed, again, again, and suddenly there was a baby just as she knew there would be, escaped out of her. Good. She and Thinlegs cut off and tied the red string between her and the baby, the same as a calf had, and what else had been inside her must now be thrown deep into the sea, not to be claimed or named.

This was a boy baby as she had decided; he cried more than Lovelove. Perhaps it was more difficult being a baby man. But Metoo had plenty of milk. Sometimes she gave a drink of it to Lovelove. Soon there were birds' eggs either to suck or to break onto fire-hot stones. Thinlegs found as many different roots and stems as she had fingers, all to be eaten. There was one which, if you chewed it, would make your throat feel good, and another which would make your stomach throw out any bad things you might have eaten.

Sometimes there were storms when people could do nothing but shelter and hope it would not find them. Hands would take Metoo and the little ones into his arms, but also he was anxious in case somehow Branch was caught by the wind. He had put strong stakes and plenty of brushwood round Branch, but as soon as the big storms were over, out he must go. With everyone looking on he uncovered Branch. They carried her down to the water, laid her in, watched no water was leaking in or not more than could be stopped, and then he and the boys and sometimes Thinlegs got into the boat, crouching on the bottom. Once the winter sheep-skins were washed out and dried and laid over the bottom, it would be easier in Branch. They went as far as the black rocks, though Catcho hated this, but Hands knew he must go that way and watch and feel the pull of the water if he was ever to do what now he wanted. From the black rocks those in Branch could see across to the new Shining which was the old where-they-came-from. Hands saw that on the times when the sea was fullest and the moon big, it seemed to push Branch away from the rocks, helping them to go where they wanted. Every time he took Branch out onto the sea he learned more about how she moved and how this could be made to happen.

On a fine day they crossed the open gap to the far land which was much like their own with even a few sheep on it which must have swum over or been carried by waves from their own place, after the lucky chance with the lambs from the first boat, which might so easily have died. There was more grass here, not so much bog and heathers. Hands thought and thought about all this. For now it was no longer the old Shining which nobody knew about and so the stories came to be made. Now it was a real place for real people. The stories had moved further. Metoo understood this and it seemed to Hands that she was making people to fill the holes in his picture.

It was about now that Metoo found a flat stone that would do for grinding. It was heavy, but the boys managed to bring it in. She tried to make a good oven, but the clay here did not want to help her, kept on crumbling. What hadn't she done? She knew by heart the words that a woman should use for her oven, but they were not working right.

Thinlegs said to Metoo that she thought Sister was now near to giving birth; but she had never become fat and strong, perhaps she was too old. The two of them went over to Sister's house where Barebum and the small boy had no notion of what it was, nor what to do, since they had never lived among people and Barebum had only been a little child when the last were born. And died. When Metoo got there Sister had become like someone a little dead, then she would wake and scream. The boy ran away. After a long time Sister screamed so loud that the baby came out of her. But then she bled and bled. Thinlegs made a drink of leaves, dropping hot small stones out of the ashes into the small crock which was all they could find.

It did not seem that Sister would have much milk for the baby, which was a girl. Metoo supposed that Hands had made the baby, so it must live. She spoke kindly to Sister, but Sister began to die. She tried to suckle the baby but it was no use. She cried and cried. But Metoo said to her 'I will feed your baby,' and picked it up and put it to her nipple. Then Sister was a little happy. But she was still bleeding too much. She took Metoo's hand and Metoo kissed her. Then her hand stopped holding and Sister became altogether dead. After the blood stopped seeping out of her, but before she was quite cold and stiff, Metoo and Thin-legs bent her so that she could lie comfortably on her side. Then they went back to their own house.

Hands had speared another seal. When he and the boys came back Metoo had now two babies, though the new one seemed to be weak, even for one that had just come out. She told them what had happened while she was cooking bits of the seal. Hands was sorry, but not very much. Only the women looked at the new baby. Metoo herself drank a great deal of the seal broth, also she said to Hands that now he must bring back food for three, since she still gave Lovelove a taste. Luckily the ewes were beginning to drop their lambs again, so there was sheep's milk and Metoo got the biggest share.

What to do with Sister? Best to take her down to the old house where the last man had been. Sister's last man before Hands. Once she was stiff it was not diffi-cult for Barebum and the boy to carry her. The others helped, mostly Catcho. There had been strong branches over the old door place. It must have been hard for Sister, dragging them there. These were pulled out so that Sister could be put in lying on her side and covered with more leafy branches. If there were other bones it was best not to speak of them. After that nobody went near, not for so long a time that the reason was almost forgotten. The two children came to the other house and ate there, better than they had done with Sister.

By now Catcho and Fishfish sometimes took the small boy out hunting with them and taught him how to use bow and arrows. You could hear them shouting at him, do this, do that, small boy! At last he shot one of the fat birds and everyone praised him. To make up for everything they gave him a big name. They called him Great Hunter. At first they giggled when they said it and so did the women, but somehow having that name was making him clever and strong.

It was also possible to snare small animals and birds with snares made from fish lines. Metoo and Thinlegs made these snares and set them. Sometimes all they caught was too small for a big meal, so it was roasted and eaten at once by whoever was there, and always Metoo with the babies. In the back of her mind Metoo began to think that if Hands and the boys took Branch over to the other Shining, those who were left would have to live on what could be snared and what this young boy could get with his bow and arrows.

Now again the time came round for planting the seed corn. But the fence which she and Sister had made was not strong enough to keep the sheep out when the corn was sprouting; so the bad parts were strengthened with stakes, the strongest they could find, put in firmly, banged down with a big stone, with long branches of hazel or alder pulled through them, in and out. Suddenly they were all laughing at a fence against sheep, not a fence round sheep against wolves. So funny! Yes, there were more sheep now. You would sight a new lamb, so clean-looking beside its raggety old mother. What pleasure to be the first to see that, to tell the others! Pleasure to see the corn growing, pleasure to find a nest of eggs. But always at the back there was now something else.

The days began to get longer and it became easier to see the other Shining in the early morning or on a clear evening. Suddenly one day Metoo said to Hands 'You will come back?' The words had burst out of her. And then she was up against him with breasts and belly and thighs and with her lips and tongue among his.

He said 'I cannot not come back. I am you.' And in a little time when he was himself again he said, 'Over there — in that Shining — it might be — another Branch. If it is known how we came.' And then he said proudly, 'It will be known,' for he saw himself speaking of it when he was there.

On a further day he looked deep at Metoo and said 'I leave you the corn,' and she nodded. She would manage — somehow. She would get the harvest. But — ah but surely, surely, he would be back with her by then!

Metoo, Thinlegs and the small boy, Great Hunter, had pushed Branch out into deep water. Barebum waited on the beach with Lovelove and the two babies. Lovelove began to cry desperately as though she had felt something bad. 'No,' said Barebum, 'No! Not gone, not gone!' She had to get a hand free to wave at Catcho, to wave him right, to wave good words to come back to her! He had given her a beautiful shell which he had found on the beach after a storm, not like other shells; he had carefully made a hole in it so that it could hang. Oh Catcho. Snuggling together in the warm sun, picking lice, feeling so close, so safe, the new name Catcho called her, Sweetlips, whispering on the sweet, warm turf and the sun sinking down on them, and now he was going, going!

The boat was moving fast, they were poling.

Catcho didn't look back at her, poor Barebum crying, no more Sweetlips. Thinlegs gave a final thrust, let go, came back dripping and shivering. Metoo rushed up onto the bank and across to higher ground where she could see, could watch them get little, little, towards the black rocks and then turn as the current sucked them out, but that was what Hands meant to happen, yes, that was what he had told her, had shown her when he had taken Branch out and near the rocks, into the beginning of the white ripple. But then he had turned in time and come back, and today it was different, now he was not coming back. Not. Not. And Branch was little, a small spot you could rub off. Branch. Hands. No! She turned and shouted at the others: 'Back, back home! Back Thinlegs, back stupid Barebum! Back, you boy!'

Metoo stayed angry for the whole day and most of the next. She had slept badly, had wrong dreams. In this bad mood she kept shouting at the other two, threw sharp stones at the small boy, who was so scared he slept out on the bare ground instead of coming into the house, and woke crying. Thinlegs shrugged her shoulders, went ahead with what had to be done, milked the ewes, taking Lovelove with her to have the first drink, filled the crock with good fresh water and sent Barebum off, snivelling, to get berries. Slowly Metoo recovered, hugged the howling babies, put one to each full breast, rocked them asleep, then set off to walk all round the shores in case — in case — but did not say it. The sea had washed a useful tree trunk on shore. She pulled it up as far as she could. There were mussel shells on it: good. Then she went to look at the field with the crop that was to make her bread. It must be all her doing now. The weeds were coming up again. But the ears were beginning to fill out. Oh, food, food. All to be thought about: planned. By her alone, without Hands. She must find some better clay to make her oven. She must look along the water at the far side. Good clay must be somewhere. More pots, they break so badly. Grass to cut. Her ears buzzed with thinking.

Barebum was keeping out of her way after she had lined her rush basket with docken leaves and then picked three kinds of bog berries, eating some. Then she began to pull away the thick hairy wisps which had been caught in the brambles and low bushes. She made a pile of it, but what could she do? She was afraid to go back. Thinlegs joined her; they went right through the wood along the paths the sheep made. How good not to be afraid of wolves, not ever any more! Thinlegs thought there was honey somewhere, she could smell it, but was scared to look for it without fire branches. You might find the tree or the hole, but bees could be as fierce as wolves. More wool. In the warm weather the sheep lost their winter wool. It came off in brownish tufts and lumps. The sheep rubbed against anything to get it off.

By the time they got back they had a big bundle of hairy wool, as big as they could carry, some not too bad, but some clotted with sheep shit. They looked at one another — why had they brought it? 'Give it to her,' said Thinlegs.

'Me — no!' said Barebum.

'I will,' said Thinlegs. 'You will see.' She found Metoo sitting on the ground looking at nothing. The babies were asleep. 'Look what we found,' Thinlegs said, holding out the big bundle.

Metoo moved her head, refusing. Then slowly she looked at the heap of yellowish-grey wool with long, clotted hairs on it. She put out a hand, then wrinkled her nose: 'It stinks!'

'We will wash it' said Thinlegs and picked it up while Metoo watched and seemed not to breathe. Barebum watched too, anxious.

Then Metoo jumped to her feet. 'Come, come, we must take it down to the water,' and then 'I have some too. Yes, me.' She had suddenly remembered the wool she had collected, the wool that wouldn't go into the pattern she wanted. It was lying under a pile of winter skins. She pulled it out. 'Dirty old wool, you wait! I can sort you. Now we shall make it all clean,' she said, and her voice had gone back to being kind and she stretched a hand to Barebum.

They all went down to the pool which the little stream made just before getting into the sea and being lost. They had made the pool bigger and put in useful stones for beating on. Sometimes a skin must be washed over and over again. They soaked the wool and all got wet, but the sun was out, warmly. When they heard Lovelove crying, Thinlegs ran up and brought her back. They beat at the mucky wool with sticks till the mess dropped out of it. The lump began to disentangle and threads of wool loosened and floated out in the water. It was no longer a lump, it could be pulled out. It looked nice, brown and with lighter shades in it.

'A stick, a stick!' Metoo sang out and Barebum jumped to get one, a long one so that they could hang the wool over it and let it drip. There was already a strong upright with a fork at the top which was useful for holding and tying. The other end of their stick was stuck in between two rocks, and the wind tossed the wool about. Metoo looked and looked without saying anything.

Her anger had left her, though she was still anxious,

going up to where she could see most of the sea and the Shining opposite and the patterns of water. But no Branch. She was still suckling both babies, though Sister's one was still weaker than her own and she began to get impatient with it. But Lovelove was now eating whatever the rest had, and a little milk from their two milking ewes. Metoo had watched the calves growing and thought the young bull had by now done what was needed on the heifer. Catcho had only cut a few armfuls of grass for winter, she would have to get some more. Both she and Thinlegs were good with a stone knife, but Barebum was little use. Still, she could gather the grass together and spread it to dry.

The wool hung on the stick all that day and the next night. When the sun was high it was still clammy, still smelled of sheep, but it seemed to Metoo that you could catch a thread, pull on it, twisting as you went, just as you might twist a heather rope. She began to do it. The thread pulled loose. She tried again. The others watched. There were harsh goaty threads and fine, soft ones, more of those, try to twist them together. Sometimes the thread broke, but sometimes small threads joined together as they had not done when she had tried with the first ball of wool. She made some long threads, longer than the stretch of two arms. Thinlegs picked one up and wound it onto a small stick. Good!

Metoo slept on what she was thinking, what had become a kind of picture, and when she woke, as soon as the babies were fed, after she had poked them to stay awake and suck faster, she went to the wood and cut two or three straight hazel sticks and peeled the bark off. She was humming to herself, not quite words. And now she was down where the wool was hanging and made more threads. The words of the humming began to come. She and Thinlegs wound the threads onto small sticks. But now, what? She tied the strongest-looking threads onto one of her hazel sticks close together. They were like the stakes of a strong fence. Then she took another thread and pushed it over and under all along the line, like you did making a fence with the springy hazel branches. There was a long tail left over. She looked at it and suddenly began pushing it back but under and over the other way as one would with a fence. That almost used up the thread. She took another and did the same thing. That went on until Thinlegs said 'Now me' and Metoo stood back to watch as the wool fence grew stronger, like a real fence when you wove the branches in and out to keep the sheep in and wolves out. But no wolves here. So it could be soft, nice! They pushed the cross-wise threads close together. There were ends of wool hanging at the sides. You could tuck them in. Or perhaps you could knot them together. If you left them they would catch and pull out. Such a lot to think about!

The two babies lay on the ground. But Sister's baby was not thriving. Thinlegs pushed it with her foot. Metoo scowled, but did not say anything. She had the same thought herself. There was nothing to be done. It was more important to make a picture of what to do next with the wool. Then a thought came to her, a picture. 'We tie the ends.' She began to do it and then saw that the wool fence would be only small. Somehow it must be bigger. In her mind it became huge, a wool fence that would cover them all, the whole of a winter, over people, over beasts. And then she had another, wonderful idea. She said to the others: 'Listen. We catch the big ewes. Two hold, one pull, maybe cut. Me, I am pulling. So much wool!' Yes, yes, exciting.

'That way is good for all our sheep. We take off their hot wool. See?'

The other two nodded, yes, yes! Do it this way instead of leaving the sheep to shed bits of wool onto brambles, clever, clever! My picture, Metoo thought, as real as a dream. 'Come! Come now!' she said to th' others, and jumped up and down. They ran, the caught one of the milking ewes. Thinlegs and Barebum held her and Metoo pulled at the thready wool which came out easily, no need for cutting. In one day they did both sheep and washed the wool. Luckily little Great Hunter had brought back some young birds from the edge of the sea which could cook over the fire, well scrubbed with leaves which put out the bad taste. Now they talked wool, wool, wool, instead of Branch.

The old man who was still looking at the sea missed his son Hands and their many days of talk together. This missing was like a bad pain in his eyes and stomach. He had began to hate the Shining which had eaten his son. He had told his people to look carefully among the bits and pieces the sea left, most of all at the foot of his own steep place. In case there was some sign of Branch. A paddle. A sheep skin floating. Or worse things. But there had been nothing. Not even after the winter gales. And he was tired, tired, and the little bird called hope that nests at the back of all a person's fears had almost stopped speaking to him.

Was it time then for him to rest his bones, which now so often hurt him, between the strong walls? He was muttering to himself over that when he seemed to see a small speck far out. It came nearer, it was now on the shoulder of the colour change, the tearing water. It was, it must be, a boat. The few that were with him peered and whispered and in a little while the whispering turned to shouting. 'Go down, down!' he said. 'Stand by!' One man ran down, jumping the bends in the cliff path, while two others helped the old man to his feet. By the time he was down by the edge of the sea, the boat was well in sight, coming into the easier waters that they all knew and it was seen that there were two men in the boat, or was it three — yes, yes, it was, Branch riding high in the water, coming in, two paddling, one with the steering oar. 'I always knew,' said the old man, totally forgetting the times when he was so certain that Hands was lost, that he would never see him again.

Now they were into shallow water and it was clear it was Hands at the steering oar. The two young men dropped their paddles to pole her in and suddenly it was as if this was what everyone had expected and waited for. The old man was there, holding out his arms to Hands, his own blood, and shouting 'Your beard has grown!' For it would not be lucky to say words of welcome and happiness. Not yet. The girls screamed insults across the water at Catcho and Fish-fish. And then the boat was over the sand strip, all jumped out and others came into the water to help her get in.

'Careful, careful!' said Hands: 'Now lift her up, up, up!' Everyone wanted to help, to get a grip of the wonder boat. Hands went over to his father, the queer feeling of steady land underfoot. 'Yes,' he said, 'my beard has grown,' and he dropped his head onto the old man's shoulder and they put their arms round one another. How strange it was, still all there. 'The

Shining,' he said, 'it is like us. It is not different.'

'Tell, tell!' someone shouted. But a woman had pushed through the crowd — she was a good pusher, Metoo's mother, clamouring for news. When she heard that Metoo was well, had a boy, she shouted back for food to be brought, quick, quick! The best! It was cow's milk and bread, good, so good. But they were all waiting for Hands, for the story. Only two or three were sad because of Catcho's friend who had drowned at the black rocks. But one of them had dreamed it, so it was half true already.

And now Hands was telling it all, telling some bits two or three times, the best bits, how he himself had made them happen; there was always someone who wanted to ask questions, who hadn't understood at first. The headman came bringing meat and some of the men's drink that was made from the women's grain. It made Hands talk even more. He told about the sheep and how there were no wolves, no bears, nothing to hurt you, and how he had built a house as good as his real house here. And there were many seals and many sea shells and plenty of fish. But he forgot to tell them about Sister until he remembered that the small boy was probably a kind of a sprig of the old man from his dead grandson, the boy who had run away. So he told about him and some of the old women remembered Sister and were sorry. But she had children. Two. No, three.

Suddenly Hands felt sleepy. He could tell them more tomorrow. The children Hands had left behind had come running round and wanted to know about their sister Thinlegs. He picked up a small one, odd to feel it in his arms. No name yet. He snuggled it up against him, older and heavier than Lovelove. The others ran ahead to get fresh water, brighten the fire and shake out the sheep skins from the bed place. He must see that Branch was safely up beyond high tide mark; no-one must touch her yet. Tomorrow he would tell them more. He was almost asleep when he pushed in to his own house. Yes, he knew it. Good. A woman who was the mother of Fishfish tried to get under the sheep skins with him, but he was altogether too sleepy and he shoved her away. And she was not Metoo. As he lay back and his eyes began to shut themselves, he felt as if he was still rocking, still holding fast to the steering oar, still watching the tide-rips, the fierce water slapping at Branch, the wave that tried to tip her, the need to shout good words to the boys. The sea-gulls had screamed at him, angry, angry. Now that he was here, why was he not there? Where was his place?

He thought it would have been nice if his mother had been there to praise him. But his mother had been dead a long time, why did he think of her? There had been a sister, the best one to play with when he was a boy, but she had fallen climbing for eggs. He thought of her too. Both of them between the stone walls. But let their ghosts come back, come back and praise him. Why could he not have that? He wished so hard for these two that he began to cry, out of his tiredness. But they were dead . . . Never came back. No ghosts. And Metoo was not there beside him. And he himself, he could have drowned at the black rocks like that boy. If you drowned you could not go to the deads' house, nor have your body folded into comfort. He had not thought of this while they were fighting the water, only now. And then he dropped down, out of this sadness into dark, good sleep.

He slept and slept. When he woke there was a hand's count of men in his house. They were watching him. His young children were peeping from behind. He reached for Metoo; she wasn't there. He blinked his eyes; it all came swinging back. One of the older men poked him with a finger and asked: 'Is it you, the same? True?'

'Yes,' he said angrily, because they were looking at him as though he was not himself. 'Yes! I was there. Now I am here.'

'So we too —— ' said a younger man and could not finish what he had tried to say. 'Yes,' said Hands, and was suddenly astonished at what he meant. 'But things to be done. Listen. The other side. It is a place for persons. But there are only sheep. And my heifer. We need pigs, goats — everything. And persons. More. Good hunters. Many more. Then we could sing. Make things. Persons who know the way of the waters. Good persons.'

They whispered. They brought him bread. So good to have bread again, to sink one's teeth in it. Cows' milk, creamy. Rich meat. They watched him eating . . . He went out of his house, sat on a rock in the sun. Licking crumbs of bread from between his teeth. Warm, good. Catcho and Fishfish came over, yawning, still half asleep, but they too had been eating bread, fresh and hot. Also they had girls looking at them and that was nice. They had not thought much about this because they had been so much afraid inside themselves, and all the time tricking and fighting the sea which could have eaten Branch, but now they began to think about what could happen if — when — they went back. One of the older men said 'We must see Branch, see her close, have fingers' feel of her, why she is so clever, can get to the Shining.'

'But it is not the Shining,' said Hands, a little angry, 'not any longer. It is like here, land. It is my other house. My new house. Better.'

'It is the Shining,' another man said. 'It is. We know. We see it.'

Why listen to this? They will stop thinking stupid things. Hands got to his feet. 'Come, we will look at my Branch.' They went down to the beach and the kindly little waves and considered Branch. There was one other boat the same size but without the long, steadying keel which, Hands knew, could somehow feel in himself, was what had kept her from tipping over when the long rip caught her, as she had to be caught to carry her where she was to go. It had made her able to ride the waves and go on her way safely. There was also the steering oar. Several boats had this, but not strong enough, he thought. Would any of them have the skill that was needed for their boat to make the great sea leap? Some talked foolishness, as though now it was easy. That was as bad as to say it could not be done.

There was one man whom Hands knew and who was certainly brave and sensible. He was called Streaky because his hair — and his beard too — was not all the same colour, but had a light streak. It was like the streaks in the sea. He was a grandson of the old man, from one of his older daughters. He had a father, still living but with pains in his joints, often angry, a no-good father. Perhaps, thought Hands, if Streaky would listen and learn? When the other men got tired, looking at Branch and listening to Hands, Streaky stayed on.

Now the girls had carried off Catcho and Fishfish. There was much laughing and screaming. The boys were forgetting about the danger, about Branch, they were being made whole and brave. Songs would be made, good words, better even than food.

Soon enough, though, the first excitement was over. People settled back into doing whatever had to be done, forgetting all this new talk about the Shining, which was still there, where it always was; they could see it. For a little time the headman had been anxious in case, somehow, all his people left to go chasing after Hands and his words, but then he saw that there was really nothing to be afraid of. Nobody could really believe, deep down, that Hands had really been where he said. Perhaps a few of the boys and girls. Still, one must be careful. It is easier to break a twig than to grow one.

But Hands had begun to plan; he was making pictures in his mind of what he intended should happen. This meant more people on the Shining, first Streaky and his boat, which must be good, almost as good as Branch. The old man had asked about the frame with the skin on it, but Hands shook his head. 'When the wind is right, yes,' he said, and puffed out a breath. 'But —— ' He shook his head, then said 'Too little wind, better to paddle; too much, nobody can hold it.' He knew he had not got the picture right. Not yet. Perhaps some time if he thought harder. 'Nobody, not even me,' he said. The old man nodded, understanding. Now he must think, think.

Meanwhile he and Streaky were away from the village for days, deep among the trees, finding just the right wood for the boat which both had in mind, for the strong steering oar and the paddles. Now Hands must remember what he had almost forgotten, to keep watch, always a little, for the sound and smell of bad beasts, the stir in the thick bushes, the small noise of claws on bark or the feet that should not be following. But also you watched for deer, always carrying spear, bow and arrows. Good to have deer meat again, deer's liver from the hot ashes, melting on the tongue. Good, good! He had forgotten. Twice he shot badly, lost his arrow. He made more, became more careful.

Streaky was angry with himself because now it came into his mind that a piece of wood which might have been just right for the new keel of his boat had come in on the end of a storm and they had used it for the big fire in the middle of the houses. It made beautiful sparks, but it could have been chipped down and turned into what now he could almost see. What stopped me thinking right, Streaky said to himself, now when I think of my new boat! Beautiful, strong. He could almost see it. Had he enough skins? He thought so but was not sure.

His wife did not want to come, no, no, she put her hands over her ears, would not listen. Her boy child had died, her girl child was too young to take. She would find another man. But in a while it seemed that her younger sister was attaching herself, would like to go in the boat. It was not difficult to make these changes to get a new man or a new woman. There could be some exchange of gifts, though certain among the older parents wanted to see big pieces of meat which would have big songs tied up with them. This girl who wanted to see new things said she could lay hands on a fine strong deer skin, right for the new boat.

Days it took. Days. Paddles. Poles. It was not only Streaky who listened. Again and again Hands told his story to most of the village so that in a way he had diminished the old story of the Shining. But this new one was better for some, it meant you could touch it. Several women edged near to Hands while he was talking. 'Go on,' they said and their fingers began to touch him and then found their way to where he had to notice. It was nice to be louse-picked by new fingers and breathed on and then followed up when the two warm parts began to melt together, to want the same thing. Nice, nice. And good dreams after, sometimes happy dreams of Metoo. Best was a woman still young but her man getting old, stiff, not wanting. This one's nipples dry and nice. Metoo so wet from babies. But still, in his mind, he talked, talked with Metoo.

This woman's children had all died except one, a boy just running about. She said to herself that if she could take him to some other place he would live, not die of winter sicknesses as the others had done. Her name was Sea-grass and she was good at making patterns on the flat sides of sheep-skins, the side you saw, and she was not easily made afraid. Would her man be angry or sad? Well, someone else could go into the house.

Hands talked to his older son who was married and settled with two small children, but found him in no mood to listen or learn. He refused to believe this new Shining story, turned his back and made ugly noises in his nose. However Hands found he had another one of his children, a boy, younger than his sister Thinlegs, who seemed clever; he had mended the roof of the house, had mended the broken leg of a young cow. He was called Quickboy because that was the name he used when he was talking to himself. It seemed he might come back with Branch. Catcho and Streaky got on well; once they began to build their boat more and more came to look and wonder. Several had scars from beasts. If you were clawed by a wild cat or bear you were lucky to become whole again. And none of these on the new Shining!

They started on the new boat as soon as they had the keel piece and the ashwood benders for the sides.

They went on during the long light days, eating at other people's fires. At last they took out the new boat. It had been a calm morning, but the wind came later, stirred up the sea. They were a little afraid, but decided to go on. The boat rode the waves, the steering oar worked well, Streaky called his boat Wave-jumper.

Two or three others had thoughts about building boats and Hands told them about the movements of the water, making pictures in the sand. The old man sat on a rock, watching him, feeling deep down that Hands was part of him, that he too had gone in spirit on Branch, that we live in our doing, but the best doing is never for one person alone, for one time alone. In the days of his hunting the old man had been part of his father's and his uncles' teaching. Even the good words of his wives as he set out with his spear and bow made them faster and surer in his hands. This was being a person, named and thought about, mixing with others and the good things they did. His bear skin had been brought down for him to sit on, in case he felt the hardness of the rock and he said to himself that he would give this to Hands when this son of his went back to the other Shining, so that, even there, talk would go on about how he had killed that bear, long, long ago.

But the headman was still a little anxious and afraid his village might become smaller, and above all that the best and bravest would go. His wife had said to him that he must speak to his brother Hands, tell him that he must not make it seem easy to get to the new Shining. She told her children that they must not listen and added that, although there might not be bears or wolves in this other place, yet there were worse things which she described to them in fearsome words:

stinging ants as long as a man's arm, huge snakes coming out of the sea. But the headman told her she must stop or these things would become real. Perhaps only a hand's count were listening and likely to go.

It was the time of longest light, but soon enough the sun would get tired of looking down. Hands began his own preparations. He had become suddenly anxious, seeing the heads of bere-barley already ripening. What was happening at the other side? Where, he thought, was Metoo now, this moment? But he had to plan. Piglets he must have. The pigs were half wild, rooting about at the edges of the forest, only sometimes driven in at night or in winter. The big boars could turn on you and kill you. But this new young son of his, who was as clever as his sister Thinlegs, picked out a litter, beginning to eat on their own. He made a basket to put them in and it began to be understood that he would go back in Branch. Streaky would take two more lambs; his family had some well-known sheep with black patches. He would also take a heifer calf and his own well-trained bitch and two puppies. A fawn? Could a boat take one? Or a kid — two kids.

The deer were half wild. They wandered and bred in summer, but it was always known where they were. You did not have to hunt for too long. It would be useful to have deer in the new Shining. They could not go away so far. But now, Hands was saying to himself, now I will take back piglets, perhaps kids, next time a fawn. There will always be next time!

Streaky would bring his new younger wife who was

eager to come, and her brother, a boy almost two hands old. Already he was saying to his older wife that he would come back and see her again later. It was as if the sea had become smaller, something with two sides. That was good. But the stories about the Shining had gone and that was not good. Something further was needed for the sake of making stories.

Two more boys wanted to come with Catcho. It seemed to him that his bad luck, when two of his friends had died, was now worn out. Perhaps Sweetlips had made him lucky again. Once three of the girls had caught him and made him do what they wanted, but somehow it was not what he himself wanted. They were not gentle and kind like poor Sweetlips, his own one. These ones were only chasing him because he had been to the Shining and come back. He knew that and it was stupid. One of them had poked him so hard it truly hurt. He had a beautiful long apron for Sweetlips, the skins of young wolves, worth two knives. One of his uncles had given it to him because he was so brave.

One bad thing happened. Boats were being thought about, if not for this year, at least for next. Someone took the hatchet which his neighbour had been using, perhaps meaning to work with it only for a short time. But he had hurried too much, had broken the handle; the stone flew off and chipped. The man whose hatchet it was became angry like a bear. They fought. Each of them wanted to kill the other. But this was something which must not happen, must not be allowed, was deeply unlucky.

Both men had the stone knives which were used against beasts, which would rip through skin and flesh. It was wrong that these knives should be used against people. The headman came running, not afraid of the fighters hurting him. Seeing him, they were bound to stop, but no. Others ran in, seized on both the men, knocked the knives out of their hands, yelled for more help, for the women to come. One of the peace-makers had his arm cut, was bleeding. And it seemed as if this was making the two men come awake and see themselves, ugly, like beasts.

They were ashamed. They knew they had been bad, but the man who had broken the hatchet was worse; he whispered to the headman, who was holding him tight, one hand across his throat, the other in his hair, that he would find and make a new handle, that he would work on the flint, at once, quickly! Both of them knew that because of how they had felt they had become like bears or wolves, had dropped from being persons. That was terrible for them. They had pains in their minds. They cried. The headman made them eat a piece of meat, bite about. Because it was very tough and everyone was laughing they too began to laugh a little. It must never happen again.

The headman spoke to them. 'There are many, many deer. There are many squirrels, there are too many wolves,' he said, 'but there are not many persons. Here we are almost many, too many for an easy count, as many as a both hands count by two hands of people. But some are children and may die, and some are old. One day our sheep might die, the cows and pigs. All, all.' Here he gave a little laugh to show he was not making a bad wish. He went on: 'Or many persons might become ill, their houses might become empty, their fires might die. All this might happen. And that is why there is a thing which must never be. When persons take up knives and try to — to kill another person. . . .'

He found it too difficult to say. To make another

person into — something for the deads' house. And yet everyone knew what he had meant to say and what was true. All came round and spoke good words to him, and put small things into his hand. His wife came running to praise him for speaking great words. If he had come later — too late — the sun might have hidden his face for ever.

Hands paid no attention, did not hear about it until evening. He and Streaky were so busy with their boats that they could not think of anything else, except that Hands was always thinking of Metoo and the harvest. But the time was coming: soon, soon. The old man came and sat with them. He felt inside himself that he wanted to go with them. To see it for himself. The Shining.

It was all they could manage, Metoo and the others, cutting the ripe heads of the bere-barley, their hands sore and bleeding from the prickles. But it had to be done, it was food for — how long? And the seed corn. They were so very few, just four persons and the un-named babies and the days beginning to shorten round them. The snares had brought in an occasional small animal at first, but either they were becoming less skilful, or the beasts were getting more wary. Or scarcer. Soon there would be another baby. It started to come, slowly, painfully. Metoo took great care of poor Barebum, as much as a mother would, more care than she had taken for the older one, Sister, who was dead. This baby sucked at first, but it was always weak and the mother's milk began to dry up. After all she was not yet full grown. Metoo made her one flat of bread. She had not meant to make until — well, better not to put it into words. For a while everything seemed to hurt Barebum, though they called her by her new name, Sweetlips. Metoo was angry with Catcho but not Sweetlips, who kept asking over and over when he would be coming back.

The heifer was due to calve soon. It was even more important that this should go right. From time to time they had cut grass and dried it. There was a fair heap inside the house. But was it enough? They pulled away some of the fencing branches and drove the beasts into the field to eat the straw and weeds as soon as they had finished getting all the grain. It had worked last time. The ewes were almost dry, but the ones that had their wool taken off them were growing new coats. They had managed to catch and pull two more, but it had been difficult. Oh, the work, the work! Metoo found herself crying in the evenings. There were no eggs now and some days only left a short time for getting shells and seaweed. There used to be such long days, she thought, at home, and not being afraid. It wasn't easy even to make a good basket here; there were no long tough stems like there used to be. Over there. The babies were not getting enough milk; they cried and cried. Her two hurt Metoo, pulling at her. She gave Sister's baby less; it got skinny and quiet; it might die. But not her own. And she herself, she was losing all her nice smooth fat, all that Hands had loved to stroke and nibble at. What would he say when — if —

Once the barley was all cut and brought in they had a few days of not working so hard, except for the boy. They sent him off as soon as it was light and he must not come back without food for their supper. It was not easy; he lost the arrows Catcho had made and he tried to make his own, but they were not as good. Even when he crawled up close he often missed. If he had got nothing by the evening he was scared to come into the house. He curled up close to the outside fire and cried. The dogs came and curled up with him. There was little for them except fish skins. You could feel all their bones. And his. If only he could be truly Great Hunter! He hated it when the women called him that, meaning to hurt. But he himself made up stories about a real Great Hunter and sometimes sang them to himself.

One day there was a bad storm. When they went down to look at the beach there was a paddle among the heaps of sea-weed and Metoo yelled with pain, saying it must be from Branch. But when she and Thinlegs looked at it carefully they decided it was not one of the ones which they had helped to shape. But it made them all sad; whose was it, what boat had lost it? After the storm there were three days so suddenly quiet you wondered how it was possible. Metoo heard the heifer lowing, thought the calf was coming, there might be trouble. She and Sweetlips went over to look. Sweetlips had left her baby lying; it hardly moved.

Yes, the heifer was in pain, standing in a bit of shelter, her udder swollen. The bull was angry, bellowing at them, but they threw stones and went to the heifer which knew them well, so that, when the calf began to show, Metoo could get at its feet and pulled. It came out suddenly in a mess of sticky blood, all over them, and Sweetlips screamed because she had never seen this and thought it had gone wrong. But the calf struggled to its feet, its dark rough hair still wet; they helped it to the cow and it sucked: another heifer. Good. Metoo sent Thinlegs running for the crock she had kept just for this — if all went well — and managed to get it half full of the first milk, enough to set. She stroked and petted the heifer and gave her an armful of the sweet-smelling summer hay. She was planning now to take half the milk when it came properly, to feed the babies, oh, if it could be done! And they must make a branch shelter for the new calf and her mother.

They ate the bestings warm as soon as it set. Metoo fed her babies and Lovelove with the horn spoon which Hands had made for her, oh, long ago in the days when she could run into his arms and he would pick her up and hold her. But the new baby would not even try to swallow it. Sweetlips was angry with it for not trying, but Metoo told her not to mind. 'You were too young. Not formed. Too small. Stupid Catcho.' But Sweetlips did not understand this. She only said Catcho, Catcho, I want him to see, oh Catcho. But the baby died. They were one less. Thinlegs took the baby and buried it in a place where the turf was easy to lift. It had never been a person. Metoo said to Sweetlips: 'Now you must stop crying. You must grow, get big, be a woman. There will be another.' But what about Sister's baby? It seemed as though it must go the same way.

And then it was the third day of the good weather. Great Hunter had gone off early. Surely, this time, he would be able to bring back something. Perhaps he would find a nest of mice. Thinlegs went down to the sea. Oh, she was tired of eating sea-weed. Treading carefully, she waded out; there was a cut on her leg that stung in the salt water, but never mind. If only she could get a fish! At last she felt one under her toes, fell on it, got her fingers round it, stood up, spluttering, shaking out her hair, her fingers tight into the gills. She looked round at the shore, how pleased they would be! A good fish, a bit for everyone. And then she looked out across the sea towards the rocks and she could see — something moving. Not seals. Not a whale. She almost dropped her fish. She stared and stared. She rushed back, splashing and shouting, calling for the others: 'Come, come!' Oh, what would they see!

They watched the boat, coming, riding in on the tide. Branch. Branch again. Metoo was crying, crying, she couldn't help it, couldn't stop herself. Hands at the steering oar, where else? Two paddling, a young boy and, yes, a woman. A big boy poling, Fishfish, not Catcho. Sweetlips burst into tears. Then they were wading out to the boat, all of them, remembering how they had pushed her out such a long time back, days and days and days, but perhaps now not really long. There seemed to be an extraordinary noise going on. Then they could see there was another big boy in the bottom of the boat who was clutching onto two piglets which had gnawed their way out of the basket where they had been caged. And all of a sudden Thinlegs knew the boy, her brother, the one called Quickboy. She screamed at him and he almost dropped the piglet which he had got by the tail.

The boat was nearly in, they reached out for her. And then Hands let go the steering oar and jumped into the sea and caught hold of Metoo, began kissing and kissing her till she almost stopped crying and began to laugh and grabbed at his beard, and he was asking what — what — had happened, why was she crying, was it Lovelove? — and why was she crying, answer, answer! But she couldn't answer, she didn't know why, she was only happy, happy, 'So what is it, what, what?' he went on, catching her close, close and wet, the tears, the cold salt water, the laughing. 'You are here,' she said, over and over, and somehow he was saying the same.

Wet work getting out all that Branch had been carrying. Thinlegs and Quickboy hugging the piglets — well, if one got loose now they were on land it wouldn't matter, it would find its way back to the rest of the litter. They must go into the fenced field until a stronger place was found for them. 'If only you'd told us,' said Thinlegs and laughed a bit shakily. The new woman had a little boy on her back and a big bundle in each hand. She was looking round uncertainly, but Metoo took one of the bundles and a grip on her hand: 'Come, come, we shall eat!' For now Branch had been carried up out of the sea, back to the place it came from, it's home. Safe, safe. Everyone was crowding up, asking questions, not really waiting for answers.

In the lee of the house Thinlegs and Quickboy were both talking, talking, trying to say everything at once, holding onto one another, each of them telling the other wonderful things — what he could do — what she had done — what had happened to the rest. The little girl, next younger — well, perhaps she could come next time. There would be another next time. Oh yes, and one after that!

There was food that day, not just the fish Thinlegs had caught — she had thrown it high up onto the sand when she sighted the boat and they all rushed down into the sea for Branch. There was milk from the new young cow to drink with the bread that had come in the boat. In the last days Hands had been terribly uncertain of what he would find, what might have happened, most of all when the gale came and it looked as if the good weather might be over — and when would it come back and what might have gone wrong over there when he could not reach to catch hold of Metoo? But that was over. He had brought a good solid sheep cheese and a smaller goat cheese, but above all there was the best of a deer's carcase and the liver sliced and bubbling on the hot ashes specially for Metoo and Lovelove. There was a small pot of honey brought by Seagrass. The new woman — what would she be like? Honey! You dipped in a straw and sucked it. Wonderful. And a good little pot, her own make. Metoo walked round saying 'Eat. Eat!' And feeling herself at last warm and full, even a little fatter.

Best of all, here was another woman admiring her house! — her big pile of hay, the skins for winter, the smell of people. Seagrass took her hand and said: 'I came when I heard you were here.' She did not make anything of being an older woman who knew more than Metoo. She could feel that Metoo was near to crying still, although now everything was coming right. Seagrass picked up the babies, but shook her head over Sister's one, shrunken-looking. 'I promised her mother,' said Metoo.

'Did you love her much?' Seagrass asked.

She answered slowly. 'No. But she was another woman.' It was something Metoo had never thought about, not till now. She went on: 'She died so I had to take the little thing, with my own. But it was never —— '

Seagrass understood. She said 'Now we are two. Listen. I had three children before this boy, the one you see. They died. I mean that this one will live.'

'I mean it too,' said Metoo, and then 'Where do we build your house? The worst wind comes from there — ' She pointed. 'We will find you strong stones. It will be good.'

Sweetlips went on crying. They told her that Catcho was to come in Streaky's boat. Streaky needed him. The other big boy who had come was a friend of

Catcho. But he was not good at speaking, he could not manage to say little things about Catcho to Sweetlips. But he made some good arrows at once for Great Hunter. They would go off the next day to try and get a seal, two seals, and smoke the meat for winter. Not the best meat but it would fill the stomach. Also there would be seal oil and, in time, seal skins. Yes, Catcho will come one day. When, when? He walked away. Not lucky to say when. But Streaky meant his boat to follow as soon as the next patch of good weather came at the right moon time for the crossing. Already this had stopped being something wonderful and frightening. Now it was real. It could be planned and thought about.

They marked out the place for the house that Seagrass would build for herself and the four-year-old. Everyone would help. It need not be a big house but should be a warm one. She had brought with her enough skins to hang over any opening. 'Three died in the dark time,' she said, 'this one — I hope for.' She had a clay lamp with a wick of sheep's wool twisted with a little pine resin. Good if the men bring back a seal carcase: plenty of oil. Metoo had two sea-shell lamps, but this one was much better. She must try to make one. Someone to help her who was good with clay! Oh, they would make pots for milk, for porridge, for meat. She was planning them already.

Hands carried up the big dark skin that had been laid as a lining in Branch. He hung it up to dry and get rid of the smell of pigs. It was heavy. Suddenly Metoo knew it — a bear skin. 'Yours?' she asked Hands. 'did you — ?'

'Mine now,' he said, and then, 'the old man came down to Branch and brought this. I told him no, he must keep it for winter. He said he would not need it. I was perhaps a little angry, told him he would be cold. But he said to me: 'It goes with you. I go with you.' That was what he said. Almost the last thing. To me.'

He had stopped speaking, and Metoo asked in a whisper: 'So then?'

'He died. Before winter came again. The old man, my father, died. He lay down and everything stopped. But he is here now. That must be so.'

She looked round, clutched at Hands: 'Here?'

'He said so. Joining with us. But he is also between the stone walls. We put him there. With his friends. Think, he must visit my brother.'

'The Headman?'

'Yes, to talk into his sleep and make him happy again now that I have taken so many away.'

'To here? To our Shining?'

'When the other boat comes we shall have great hunting. We shall be almost many persons. But no bears. Perhaps that is why the old man gave me the skin.'

Metoo thought this over and ran her hands through the bear's thick coarse fur. Then she said: When summer comes you must catch all the sheep so that I can take the wool off them.'

'Why?' he asked.

'That is a thing I will show you,' said Metoo, 'in the bed place.' And then she thought to herself of her new picture of how to make the wool fence, in and out, but not so that the stick stayed with it always, but like she saw it now, in her mind, with a strong, strong cord of wool instead. It would be difficult but she knew she could do it. So when at last Hands had seen the wool fence, picked it up and stroked it, looked carefully to see how it was made and all the time said good words, soft, warm, clever, she knew that the next one would be better. Would most certainly be better. He had put his finger through it and she had smacked him, but not hard. And then the full picture jumped at her. If there was no stick holding it? Yes, then I could throw it round myself. Or round Hands. Or over Lovelove. And it could all be pulled tighter, closer.

And when this other boat comes we shall be three women. I shall like that. I will show them how to make a wool fence. Even if Sister's baby dies, as I think it must, there will be more. Perhaps Thinlegs will like one of the new boys. And poor little Sweetlips can have Catcho again. Next time she will be bigger, stronger. We will have a good fire-pit and make strong pots and a better oven. We will fill the pots with barley. We will make cheese. We will find honey. We shall make more fish lines. This new woman Seagrass, who will be a good sister for me, she says she makes patterns on skins, yes, I remember when I was still young, over there. Perhaps she will make patterns on our houses. Or even on a wool-fence. One day, she said to herself, I shall go back to the old Shining, I shall wear my wool fence wrapped all round me and it will be all colours like the flowers that come suddenly all together when the dark times are over. And I shall walk in the old Shining, but I will know that this is the real one, this is the one we named.

So, what happened? Well, the other boat got over safely and poor Sweetlips got her Catcho back. There was another boat, not so well made, which was sucked into a current, turned over and smashed, but that was only known many months afterwards. Now those who had crossed safely were getting beyond a family, but still close, mostly eating together. In a year or two another boat managed the crossing. One of the Headman's children, disobeying everything his mother said, got himself into that boat and joined his cousins. Did Metoo ever go back to walk proudly in her old place? Not as she pictured; and she never went far enough with her wool game, because there was always so much else to do. Yet her idea was bound to come up again whenever there were sheep and brambles to catch their wool. In the settlement Metoo was thought of as the one who must always be consulted and listened to; she was wise and clever as well and in spite of having several more babies, most of whom lived, she went on for a long time, more than twenty years from the time we know her. She never counted them. Proudly she saw her grandchildren making sand castles and finding their own berries and shells. Hands had died in her arms and been put under the earth, but somehow she knew he was not really dead, for he still spoke happily in her dreams.

That settlement grew and there were other settlements. People got to understand the ways of the sea better every generation; they were passed down from father to son, as by Catcho and, rather better, Quickboy. There were difficult years when too many died, but still there were always enough child-bearers and food-finders for the spread family to keep going.

Later more crossed and some from the first settlement had moved, even adventuring across a smaller bit of sea, swimmable on a summer day, to find another place and unused pasture for the beasts. It was found that it was a good idea to exchange things between groups. If you could have more beasts than you could keep over winter or salt and smoke for food, and some other group or family were good at making knives or axes and had the right kind of stone to flake off, answering to what it was told to be, then you met, ate and drank together and made a bargain that was a pleasure to both. There would certainly be some kind of pots which were better than others, perhaps because the clay had some special kind of material in it or because they were better made and decorated. Other women would want those pots and would bring something else in exchange.

But it was not only things that were exchanged between groups. The young people looked at one another. Here was something new and interesting, not what you knew all about and so didn't want. No, no, this was fresh as spring flowers, as bread straight from the baking! And so there would be exchanges between families. And also between genes. The strong ones lived.

Surely, however far back we look, men and women like to decorate themselves and one another. They try out all sorts of ways, coloured earths, plant and berry juices, little knife cuts, beads and dangles. There must have been games, racing, hopping, throwing, or playing with different coloured stones; there must have been fun with words. New words would be invented; sometimes they were passed on, sometimes not. There were songs that matched up with what people were doing. There were ways of making nice sounds. And time went on but nobody thought of catching and marking it. Everyone wanted good times with the right amount of sun and rain, plenty to eat, good songs, plenty to burn for warming and cooking, babies coming easily, nobody hurt or dying.

But there seemed to be no way of making sure of good times. So people began to make up stories about it. There were people who watched and seemed to know when bad times were coming. You remembered something they said, some way they moved heads or hands, some look. There must be twisty ways of hiding from bad times. There might be one person who could tell you the way, who would make a little light so that the dark would go back into corners. Oh the dark, the winter dark and perhaps this time it would stay, it would not be driven out, unless — unless — if you hurt yourself a little it might stop a bigger hurt? That must be true. It was in your bones. If one person was hurt — badly — might that do for everyone? Difficult questions floated up from the dark. Where have we come from? Why? There was a story that some people liked to tell themselves. In this story the sea eagles caught a fish in their strong claws, a fish that had a person inside it, or perhaps was a person. Also there were certain things which if you ate or drank them —

but not too much — you would be strong, you would know you were winning, could push back the dark, live for ever. Yes, there were ways of getting help. The dead could be made to come back, to speak to you. Or be silenced.

All this would build up over the generations and through stories, becoming something you could almost see and touch. Somebody would, perhaps suddenly, perhaps after many summers, become aware of a power in themselves. Then others would hear whispers, see something not ordinary. And so it would grow. Some natural objects, some animals, some birds, would become larger than life, would be turned over in dreaming and make fear come and stand at your back. How to catch this fear and kill it?

But hundreds of long life-times would go by while all this was churning and floating in people's minds, when fears changed shape slowly or suddenly. Sometimes people thought of new ways of doing things and perhaps they were copied or perhaps not. And in time there is this girl child called Little Honey playing around the low, dark houses which centred on — what? — or in the sunny fields and middens, or helping to pick up sea things at low tide, or good leaves. Now she is getting stronger and taller. Strong enough, her mother thinks.

So there was Little Honey wanting to be outside. She wanted to be far, like a bird, swimming in blue air. That was new. She had nearly always been inside. When she was a bairn her mother had taken her out to the fields and sat her down between great stones which were like the comfortable fatherly stones of the house itself. She could help as soon as she was old enough, gathering up the fallen ears of the short barley, or later, carrying the brown weed up from the shore to feed the land. The land ate the kind of sea stuff that people did not care for but sheep would bite at. But she never went far, not out of the smell of the house.

The house smelled of people and sometimes it was the big-man or his brother who was nearly the same. Strong is what they were, they would pick you up and whirl you by the hands. They had a special smell which she liked, but sometimes it was more the smell of her mother and that was different at different moon times and also because her mother was a potter and sometimes there was the hard, cold smell of clay. There were two bairns, littler than she was, one a boy able to throw stones, the other a tottie-wee girl-thing, but lively. She half remembered others, the one that coughed and coughed and got so thin its bones showed all over and that other, not right, could never stand properly, so the rest were always knocking it over and laughing. Both of them were buried under the hard earth floor of the house, so that they could catch a mother and be re-born. She herself, her mother said, was born again from one before who had been buried, but she did not remember this. She had forgotten dying. All that was part of the house-talk. She did not think it outside.

In winter it was best to stay in behind walls if you could. But if there had been a storm you had to go with the rest to see if the sea had brought gifts for houses, maybe something for the fires, or a big fish with its shoulder bitten off by a seal, or even a seal itself if they had been fighting. The old ones sat round the fires, their front parts warm. When you brought the drink you did not look too close, not at least at the grandfathers who might pull you down to warm them more. It was all right when you were a bairn and nice to be warm, but as you got big you liked them less, least of all the ones with teeth that wanted their meat chewed for them. Better to keep warm among yourselves, and there was play and dancing and jumping and swinging, all to make you warm. But it made you hungry too and that was good if there was food, but bad if there was no food.

The Big Woman who was also the Good Woman had a fire to herself so that the whole house was warm. The stones felt warm when you leant up against them. The bairns huddled warm in the corners. Your mother had been one of the Big Woman's bairns until something had got into her and she began to swell and then there was a father and so it went on. The Big Woman threw them out when they were got this way and then they must find a place inside other walls, maybe even the new walls that had bad winds which could blow through, blowing away the warm and the smell of people. But out here they found other mothers and learned from them, not the Big Woman's singing and sliding and shouting, but things of comforting use. If there were too many bairns the Big Woman would need to feed the eagles and there would be a strong smell of what was making bubbles in the great trough, with herself leaning over it and the striped beads of eagle claws swinging from her neck and into the trough almost. Then all the people would drink and dance and fall over and there was the noise of the horns that called back and back to the bulls they had been once; and the bulls came out of the dark and then the eagles came and their wings swished but you could not hear it any longer nor yet what might be screamings and sobbings and crunchings because of the noise of the bulls. So it was right that the Big Woman, who was also the Good Woman, should have a fire of her own, and smoked meat and fish hanging and more grain pots than you could count.

Also the Big Woman was not afraid to go alone to the high rock above the sea and when the full moon, which not everybody cares to look at for more than a glance, came over a certain place and the stars that served the moon had come behind her, then it was time to take up the digging sticks and sow the seed. That also meant that the lambs would drop; she ordered this. The Big Woman would take a lamb, that was her right; without her to call the moon up it could be dark all night and every night.

The year before had been bad, bad. The sun had looked coldly, dark had been cold and windy and wet. Half the lambs had died and two calves out of the six.

The same with the dogs. There were only handfuls of grain left which would hardly last until harvest. No gorging of bread. Meanwhile everyone needed to gather what they could — fish and sea things and roots. The sea birds' eggs were best but a boy had been lost climbing. The sea had got him. No pots were made that year; they would have been sure to break.

The Big Woman knew all this but she told them it would pass. She was the Good Woman and so she knew. She told them that the eagles would soon be bringing them a gift, and so it was. One day when they went down to the beach there was a big tree with branches floating only a few feet out, so that it could easily be brought in and used for things that wood is meant for, axe handles, plowing poles, rods and bars and skin stretchers. The small branches were broken for firewood. The fires mostly ate the turf but they liked best to eat the wood out of the sea that made coloured sparkles and shapes. The Big Woman had a stack of sea wood for her own fire and she was never alone by it. That would never do.

In a good year the potter mothers came in to her house to have what they made handled and put over breasts and made into new pots for their family. If some of the small bairns had grown and become people they too would be brought for the same thing to happen to them. All must be touched by the Big Woman before it was right for its purpose. The men or boys might bring killers and crushers, shaped and hammered stones with thin sharp edges or good hand holds. Some were shaped so that they could be tied to handles with strong strips of skin. The Big Woman might take one if she fancied it. But the house builders waited for the Big Woman to come to them. They were proud and bearded, had lowered and dragged the great dead stones out of their nests, their own arms and backs almost, it seemed, cracking, but always to be put right by warmth and women. It seemed to the girl bairn that their big-man was one of these — it was he who had called her Little Honey.

So one way or another the Big Woman who was also the Good Woman was aware of everything. There were people like the fingers of two hands counted over finger by finger and then counted again and after that sometimes again, but after a bad year, not. These were the grown people, the persons of the houses. And two hand finger counts would take in the old ones who were useless except for telling stories and the small bairns who might or might not go on living and had not yet been named. Food was not always spared for these ones, not in bad times. It was best if they died and then they could either take themselves far off or be born again. But only the Big Woman could tell over that.

Sometimes there were not so many even of the strong ones if it had been a bad year, when legs and arms became thin and there was coughing and belly pain, and some lay down to go back into the earth. It had been a good year when Little Honey had come with her mother to the Big Woman who had fingered her and slid kisses about her and hummed into her ears. It had been wonderful and terrible but she had not let herself go in fear. So in the end her mother took her back and she was pleased and made Little Honey into a song, and after that said no, she was not to go into the fields, she was to learn pots and become a real person. And so it came about, for a good year followed the bad one: lambs, calves, kids, farrowing sows, strong growth of barley.

The potter women spoke and nodded and thought

what to do on a time of sun and wind when the sea was ruffled but not raging. Black turf had been pulled out and left to dry. The potter women shoved it about to dry better for what they needed. More people were moving about outside the houses, looking at the beaches for what could be found, wading out for the shells, fishing from the rocks, worrying about the young lambs. The potter women came out from the houses, though one of them was ill and could not come; her bairnie had come too quick and had died and she was still bleeding and crying. Her pots would have cracked. But there were two new young ones and Little Honey was one of them. They sang special songs quietly. So there she was outside but not bird-free: she was a learner. She and the other did not know where they were going, only that it would be far, but they were safe, they were with their mothers and they were to become potters.

Yet the pots whose shape the women were beginning to see at the back of their eyes, were still far off. First they must get the clay, the mother stuff. There were two springs up in the hill and as the water made its way down, so there was clay, brown and slippery. They clawed their way into the banks, down under the turf edge; the two learners were shown how to get out all the bigger stones and roots. There were deep holes under some of the banks and yet there was plenty left. How? Always. The women had an ox-hide with them and they filled it with clay lumps which they felt for carefully with their hands. It was heavy before they had finished but four men had come to carry it back across the hill to the place which had been named by the women. One of them was Little Honey's big-man and they nodded proudly to one another. The men knew themselves honoured to be chosen for this women's skill, which men had never taken part in, not having been given the right knowledge. They took it where the women said and laid it down and left without looking in case they saw something they should not have seen. Here the clay dried out and the women picked it over to take out stones and bits of stick, singing a special song. The two learners joined in, at first under their breath and then properly. They knew they had taken the first step towards something special, for themselves alone.

This was a whole day's work beyond the houses. When they went back inside the walls it seemed to Little Honey that the house was squeezing and pushing the outside away from her, covering her with the inside smells. No, no, she must keep the outside. She fought it with the potters' song at the back of her throat. She was outside again in her dreams.

The weather held and the clay waited. The next thing for the potter women was the digging of the fire pits and lining them with the turves which had been cut long ago to be ready for this. These were old pits filled in again and again, so not too hard to dig. The two learners clawed away with hands and digging sticks. One was the great fire pit and the other was its child, the small pit. Little Honey wondered, but knew she would get the answer. The turves must be raised a little on stones, or they would not burn right through, evenly. All took time but every morning when they went back this was real and the inside only a place for a quick cooking and sleeping. The big-man did not visit, but left meat where it could be seen.

The clay must always be worked; they went on, squeezing it through the fingers and taking out the tiniest bits of stone or stick or grass. Some lumps were a little different from others, it was something a real

potter woman must get to know. But there was more
to it than that, as with the forming of a person, not
only inside the mother but while it was outside but still
too small and soft to be shown to the Big Woman and
made properly into a person.

So at first Little Honey copied what her mother did
with the clay and when she went wrong and tried to
hurry it her mother stopped singing and the quiet hurt.
Next she learned how to break up the bits of old
already broken pots and beat the bits with a stone
hammer till they were dust. Unless the old dead pots
lived again in the clay the new pots would not live —
they would crack before they were taken from the fire.
Little Honey kept watching and remembering everything. Her mother had her tools beside her, things
which were kept in a hide bag hung from a stick in the
cracks of the stone wall, and must not be touched, the
shells that were either cutters or scrapers or with the
smooth roundness outward, smoothers and pressers.
Yet sometimes a fingernail was the best, or you might
use a lamb's bladder blown up and tied, good for
shaping.

Little Honey liked to roll the clay between her
hands. It moved, it became long, it was made to curve.
Another was laid above it with stroking and smoothing and then another; it rose into a pot shape. At first
she could not make the rim into the clean full-moon
shape as her mother seemed to do without effort. But
she saw the shape so clearly in her mind that at last,
after three days, she found she had it right and after
that it went mostly as she wished. By now her mother
had stopped hitting her or making angry noises.
Instead she made Little Honey put her voice into the
potter's song and also she showed just how to use the
shells to make the marks which were the signs that the

potter had truly handled and given life to her pot.

There was more to be done. Before the clay at the base of each of these pots that they had made hardened into something like a tough hide, the pot must be up-ended. Then it must be nursed upon the lap, while the first thick clay ring was squeezed thinner without losing its shape. At last, with one hand inside the pot and the other outside, the ring was made to join together. Now the pot was itself. After that the marks could be made, clothing it all round, each woman making her pot children a little different from those of her neighbours, so that she could know them and speak to them in their working life, even if they were in another house.

While the clay was drying in the sun and wind, there was yet another thing for the women to do. A few of the best pots would be put to lie in the small pit beside the long fire pit. This was thickly lined with the smooth damp leaves of yellow iris and the crinkled soft young fronds of bracken. But they must be mixed with enough really dry leaves, bits of heather and tufts of wool, to make sure that the green stuff was so heated that it would smoulder into ashes. The lining of that important pit was made with some arguing and shouting by the potter women and Little Honey among them.

Then came the lighting of the fires in the long pit from their carefully sheltered fire pot that had been blown into by the oldest woman. The leathery pots had been placed, propped against small stones and with more turves piled all round them and at last on the top, their softer sides down so that nothing could mark the pots and all could be heated evenly.

From the time of the working of the clay until the last of the firing, it had taken more days and nights than could be counted on one hand. But none of the potter women went back inside the walls even on one night of rain when they pulled the big ox-hide over one another and slept close as seeds in a pod. They were short nights. The sun dipped but the moon took his place and they thanked her, standing. There was the sea ripple and the wind in the grass. Sheep and cattle were within smell. A fox barked. In the place where these people's folk had come from long, long ago in the skin boats, there had been other night things to fear. There had been wolves and bears; by now it was said that in those days they were two-headed, with teeth as big as trees. Or other man-eating terrors had been dreamed of and told about so that they became real. Such terrors were always kept by the Big Woman to be taken out if need be, if fear had to be wakened and felt. But always the old terrors must be torn and abolished by the great terror of the eagles.

You could see that far land mostly on late summer evenings when the sun's last light came on it. It did not look frightening. Sometimes a boat came over from there with a few people on it, always in good weather and when the moon was halfway between new and full. These people spoke like they themselves did, or almost. They had good things with them, skins of bears and foxes, good knives, good arrow heads. But it was known that their pots and beads were not so good. So there was always a trade to be made at these times by the potter women. They would manage three or four firings and store whatever pots they thought best to pass on.

Sometimes too the people from over there asked for a girl and if the Big Woman said yes they would take her and then they might leave as much as the silky pelt of a wild cat or even a bear skin. But the Big

Woman would never give one of the potter girls. Even if she wanted to go and went over there she would never be able to make good pots with their clay, for it was not like their own clay from their own clay bank. So the Big Woman would send a girl from another house and she was not to go unless she fancied the man who wanted her, though sometimes if one went a sister might follow.

Next time the boats came across it might be told she has had a child by such and such a man, is fat and singing. That would be good. Or dead: not good. Those people had big trees to make the frames of their boats, long branches that they bent so cleverly, not like the birches and hazels, the bending willows and wind-broken small pines that the Good Woman who was also the Big Woman grew for her people. Perhaps the people on the other side had a Good Woman who grew big trees. You did not ask.

It was also told about the Other People that they did not live on the far land, but across the little waters that a man could swim. One could sometimes see their fires or the drift of smoke from behind a hill. It was said that they were brave. They made good boats and caught big fish. They could shoot the birds out of the air. But they did not grow corn or make porridge or bread. It was said that they could speak with the deer and that they understood about plants. But their talk, though it sounded at first like real words, was never spoken the right way as they themselves spoke. If one of the Other People came, as happened now and then, but perhaps not for years, he might ask for a girl, but the Good Woman would not give. So if he stole? Sometimes the girls thought about this and it made them feel funny inside, but they did not speak of it, not in words, though one would know what the other was picturing. But the two potter girls had now so much else to be thinking of.

Two boys were fishing late from the rocks below the hillside of the potters. They had caught saithe, one they were eating raw in case they got little when they took the catch up to the houses. They could see the far land from there, but nobody saw it from the sheltered banks where the potter women slept, spread over with a sweet cover of white and yellow sun-warmed flowers. The two girls learning from their mothers smiled at one another, but stayed apart, for at this time each must only set herself on the skill of her mother. The potters had brought two big rounds of barley bread and some drink in one of their own bowls, but they gave none of that drink to the two girls. They were only given little corners of bread, but they could eat any roots they could find without going out of sight and at the good time of the sun's light. They must not see any persons but potters. Little Honey wanted to go down to the sea to look if there was something to eat there, but her mother grabbed her hard and stopped her and afterwards made her sleep close beside her. But at least she had the taste of daisy stalks and the sucked honey from the clover heads to turn in her mouth. And so the last night went on and the cold slow dawn of middle summer. After all, everyone was used to going hungry for a day or two. But near the fire pit the ground was warm. The potter women spoke quietly among themselves. Yes, it was time to open; they knew just how to do it. The girls watched, aware of every movement of their mothers' hands.

The turves had burned through but the pots were too hot to touch and there was a shimmer over them, a life. Was it possible that this time all the pots would come happily out of their forming and birth place?

Wait, wait. The women touched the pots gently with plant stalks, dockens or bennyweed. One pot moved, cracked. The potter woman who had made it said something quickly under her breath, spat to right and left. The rest of the pots seemed to have become what was meant. All breathed deep, nodding at one another. If a pot was not too badly cracked you might mend it with holes carefully drilled and a thong put through and tied. It could do for many things, but not to be shown to the Good Woman.

Each of the mothers named one or two of her pots to go into the small pit with the leaf lining. These were round bowls, but two had their rims pulled into a neck and then the neck pulled up a little and the mouth finger-smoothed at one side of it. That was a new kind of thing. It had meant difficult smoothing in the narrow space inside. But two women, one of whom was Little Honey's mother, had been very quiet, working on this until it had seemed right. This also had meant more space for decoration, and one of these had stripes and dots that set off the new shape, the other had narrowing rows of nicks. Now these seven pots had to be moved from the long fire-pit into the leaf pit. They were very hot. They quivered with heat. But the women — or perhaps their mothers or grandmothers — had made a way to pick them up safely. In storm time bits of trees were broken off on the far side and carried across; sometimes even there would be a suitable branch on one of their own small wind-blown trees which could be trimmed into shape. It must be a strong and long branch, almost straight, but at the end it must have small branches sticking out which could be pushed under the pot to lift it. This end must be soaked in water so that it would not go on fire from the hot turves and the hot clay. The older sticks were much blackened because of this. All had to be tested. If they broke it would be terrible. Two women worked together to lift each pot over into the leaf nest. The two girls watched, fists clenched and mouths open with excitement. But all went well; more leaves which had been picked and put ready were piled in between and over the red-brown shapes. Black smoke came up in clouds, it stuck to the fingers, damp and steamy. Then a sheepskin was pulled over the leaf pit to keep the smoke in, and earth piled on its edges.

In the big fire pit the turves were now totally burned through. The pots lay in the ashes and there they stayed till the next day. All the women slept that night in the warmth round the pits, sometimes smelling the smoke that seeped from under the sheepskin over the smouldering leaves. All slept well, aware of what they had done and the extra goodness they now felt in themselves. There had been a little rain that night, but nothing to wake for. Little Honey's mother, only half awake, pulled the edge of her ample apron, a dressed and decoated sheepskin, over Little Honey's shoulder and back. The girls still wore nothing in the summer but narrow strips of whatever animal skins were to be had. But they were always making for themselves and one another necklaces of whatever they could find, feathers and seed pods and shells and twists of wool. Two of the potter women had made some beads with the left over clay, some had been put into the leaf pit. They would be for the two new potters.

Morning, and time to lift the warm pots. Another of them had a crack. It always happened — me last time, you this time. Perhaps the clay had been angry, perhaps you stopped your song too soon. Or the clay was just playing. Never mind, it would be all right next time. The two learner girls admired the pots, especially their own mother's. They knew all the same that they would be kept burnishing them with the stone for many days after this. They had done that last year but now it would feel better to do it since they knew the pots, most of all their own ones. Each of them had two, but Little Honey had a special one she had worked on until she was totally satisfied with its shape, and then decorated, slowly, with her mother's shell cutter, able to breathe as she made the patterns, oh good, good! She had hardly dared to put it into the fire pit, just in case it might crack.

Now there it was, not cracked, standing among the ashes, hers. She took a deep breath. She would be so careful of it. Always. She would look at if often. But there was work still to be done. She knew that. Some of the pots would have to be filled with milk which must be left to sour and sink in; after that the pot would hold water but it would spoil the burnishing a little, so that it must be done again. But if it was to be a grain pot or seed pot then it would not ask for the milk.

One of the cracked pots broke altogether when they lifted it. Never mind, the clay would live again in another pot. And then they pulled the sheepskin carefully off the leaf pit and Little Honey pushed through sideways past her mother and saw the beautiful gleaming black pots which had eaten and decorated themselves with the smoke. What skill, what satisfaction! Enough for a small trade. There would be more. The makers nodded at each other, feeling filled as with a meal of good meat. They put the pots out on the turves, shifting them this way and that, almost playing games with them. They were still as warm as the hands that touched them, but cooling in the wind. At last it seemed that the word had gone round. Others had come out of the houses and there was praise and singing and giving of small gifts. The two girls wore the new beads, strung onto thin strips of leather. The big-father-man who had helped with the hide had cooked fish for Little Honey's mother, who ate it at once but gave a bit to her daughter who was now a potter like herself. The other girl potter had a roast bone with plenty on it. Both of them were holding their own pots which they had made, sucking in the sweet words of praise. Little Honey's mother licked her fingers and let her big-man put his hand under her apron. Everything had gone right. Tomorrow they would see the Good Woman.

But when she heard that said, Little Honey knew she didn't want it. Nobody had told her. No. No. When her mother had said she must give her first pot to the Good Woman: for the eagles — no, again no, she had pulled away clutching her own best pot which she had made herself, her pot child. Must she? Must she? Yes, her mother had said, because if not — the eagles —— And her mother's face wrinkled, she could not go on, she did not have the words to say it; she would show her own pots, but not give them.

The potter women began to go back into the houses to be with the whole of the praising people. Warm and good they felt and now some of them were turning to their own man among the praising men, who would do even better than praise, better even than a full meat meal. There was singing. There was thumping on drums and blowing between grass blades or into shells. There was the smell of people, you could sink down into it. If you were one of the potters it was understood that you had made, were making, all this; you were proud. It was good, it was warming to be proud.

But Little Honey who had been so full of the picture of her pots could not bear it. To give her own pot-child to the smell, to the dreadful dangle of eagle claws, how could she? The other learner girl was huddled in a corner, over her own best pot — but not as beautiful as mine, Little Honey thought. That one was crying a little, she would do what she was told. But I — but I — Then suddenly her mother had come up behind her and whispered: 'You must. You must. Hold back is bad — bad. For you. For us. The eagles will know.'

How could her mother do this? — her mother who had taught her, praised her, watched her make this very pot! 'No, no!' she growled back, but her mother had suddenly caught and twisted her hair, was pulling her up, onto her feet, the pot still clutched. She and the other learner were herded along through the crowd, the singing and drumming. She knew at the bottom of her mind that if she tried to dodge away they would catch and hold her. Laughing at her. They knew where she was going, and why. Some of them grinned and touched her, nastily. And then she was pushed through the hide curtain and into the smell.

It was difficult to see. The light hole showed some things but not others. There was plenty you could not want to see. The sound of voices and drumming came and went like waves. The Big Woman walked towards them slowly, her face fixed, her high wooden shoes making a clomping noise. She bent over them and their pots and the eagle claws moved and rustled and both learners were crying as they held out their pots and saw that something was being poured from high up, perhaps the sky, into each one. The arms of the Good Woman were round them and her voice whispering, drink, drink.

The taste was like honey gone bad, but there was something else — what? The Good Woman had picked leaves, found roots, spoken to the eagles, her eagles. When Little Honey woke up it seemed she was lying on her own skin mat on the straw heap of her own house and her mother was beside her, her mother who had forced her. Now she was inside, back in houses, between stones, among people. No more outside. She shifted, turned her back, felt a bit sick, and also became awake, sore here or there. As though bits of her had been pushed through a bramble bush. She put up her hand to her face. There seemed to be a sore kind of line on it, all along one side. As she groped at it, still in a muzzy anger, she felt another hurt, but lower down. She felt for that too, came up with blood on her fingers. How? Why?

She felt her mother turning her round, giving her milk to drink. And then this mother of hers pushed back her own hair and Little Honey could see that she had a scar line, a little simple line, from the end of the jaw to almost the eye corner, the same place as her own now. Somehow Little Honey had never noticed this; her mother's hair had always half covered it. Unless one looked. After all, most people had small scars from falls or sore places, why not. But this was different, this was on purpose. And the other hurt? Her mother's hand followed her own down and it was clear, oh yes, that her mother knew that one as well.

She began to sit up, felt sick and dizzy and horribly afraid. But her mother's arm was round her and the answer that there was nothing to fear, all had gone well. 'But what?' she asked and the whisper came back: 'the eagles, the eagles.'

Nothing made sense. Sleep came over her again and this time she dreamed back into outside and the lifting of the pots — her pot, her own pot. She looked into her mother's eyes and asked 'Where is it?'

'She has it,' her mother whispered, 'to keep. Because this has been done. So that you become strong.'

'Me? By her? No — no —— '

'Strong to be a potter woman. Eagle-strong. She makes it.'

'A potter woman?'

'Yes.'

'Then — am I clever? My hands good? Say, say!'

'Good, good. Clever. Good hands. Good like mine. Now I give you a good stone. Best stone. We must finish the pots. You know.'

Yes, thought Little Honey. She had known that some of the pots must be properly burnished, made to shine. She knew the way to do that. Sitting in the sun.

'Outside,' she said, and now she stood up, only just feeling the sore bits of herself. 'I must go. Away from houses.'

'Yes,' said her mother, 'but you come back.'

Little Honey had no answer, not yet. She went out from the house and the air was bright with sunshine and she could hear the lambs, plenty of lambs this year, plenty of ewe's milk cheese. Four or five boys were herding the pigs, keeping them off the barley on the places where good leaves and roots were growing. Two broods of piglets. She could hear them squealing. The barley field looked good, but she was not one to bend her back weeding, no, because she was a potter. Different. Better. She went on and up the hill, out of sight and smell of the houses. There was land and then there was sea, sea, drowning or bringing gifts and beyond it other places, the far place across the difficult sea, but if you looked the other way, near land coming like clouds out of the sea. Out there were people in houses: living there, speaking.

She knew. The men went there sometimes in the boat that belonged to their own houses and came back with stories or with things that they had got in exchange. And I, Little Honey thought, I might go that way, far, far; I could carry my pots and they would praise me in far off places. I could make pots there. Because now I have the skill. She thought of the lost pot and, hazily, of the Good Woman and the bad tasting drink. It seemed a long way back. Her next pot would be better, she could see it.

For a time she lay on the ground, nibbling at good leaves and shoots, and thinking that she would go far, far. The air opened in front of her. Because she had something inside herself which was the shape of pots and how to make the shape come. Shapes. And then sleep came on her again and she shut her eyes and let the sun warm her all through.

So what did Little Honey do? Well, she still had more to learn about making pots. Oh, much more. When you have learned the beginning of something skilled and know you will be able to do it well, you will want to go on. Perhaps when the pots were being exchanged with things from Outside, she might make a big jump and go away with them; if one of the Outside people wanted her and spoke sweet words and made promises, this might have happened. But who knows? One day she would have a daughter of her own to teach, and then again that daughter would pass it on. And long, long times go by and changes you can hardly notice at the time make the patterns of living go another way. If the skill dies out, it is likely that another will come into being. In his time Hands could not think of a mast for his boat, although he understood how a kind of sail would make it go quicker; but someone else must have thought of a mast, perhaps many generations later. When most people die young they escape the pains and worries of old age, but they have very little time for inventing things and passing them on.

And now, we begin to have clear ideas about what

is going on, even in the northern islands. In warmer, more fertile lands, cities have been built, religions have been established, water has been led to dry land, useful and beautiful artefacts are being used and traded. People know about numbers and marks of ownership. They know about the movements of stars and when an eclipse may come. They trade with one another, but if they want more than they can get by trading, they make war of some kind, although some large groups of people seem to have done without it.

So they have the makings of history. Further south they are already using first copper and gold, then bronze, even the beginning of iron. There have been migrations of people over great distances. But in Orcadia where there are no easy minerals, we can catch only the beginnings and these beginnings are not quite history, although they are the stuff out of which history will be made. The people here live in a place where I have been myself, on the edge of the sea, now called the Eagle Tomb. Here I have to be very careful of treading on the toes of the archaeologists. One of the great pleasures and excitements of archaeology is building up theories out of the evidence, but yet this evidence may not always offer a clear interpretation. In fact it very seldom does. But look at the interpretations that we make on our own society, not only differing but antagonistic.

Over even the recent periods, in my own life time, there have been differing fashions of archaeological interpretations. The version I have made up here is not a very probable one, but it seems to fit into some bits of evidence, though perhaps not the majority. Feelings about the dead vary enormously from one culture to another. In the course of a lifetime which has included a fair amount of travel I have been in friendly sympathy with views and actions which I do not share myself. In the days of that splendid African traveller, Mary Kingsley, there were even more marked diversions from European custom. It is good to think she took them in her stride.

It appears that, throughout Orkney, only bones, not bodies, were laid in the stone tombs, or whatever we choose to call them. Perhaps not even everyone was so treated, but only the important and their families. We just do not know. In any case the flesh must vanish before the bones can be entombed. There are or were no large carnivores in Orkney. But a lightly buried body or a body covered with branches or turf will be bones after a year or two, and possibly they had different feeling about the smell. I doubt if the sea-eagles, whose claws are so much in evidence at the Isbister tomb, were much help in cleaning the flesh off the bones, but yet they had some function, whether real or symbolic, perhaps a way of frightening people. Eagles of one kind or another seem to occur in the background stories and emblems of many cultures.

Each of these Orkney tombs — or admiration places, fear places, pride places — seems to have been built within a fertile piece of land, usually close to the sea, the great giver of food and useful bits and pieces. This amount of land and beach could feed a large family group of people, young and old. But clearly they must be on good terms with their neighbours.

It is possible that there was a little more fertile or grazeable land than there is now. It may be that the great terrifying cliffs close to the Eagle Tomb with the sea ranging and breaking away below, were distinctly further away than they are now. It seems that the sea breaks off several yards a century, or even more if there is protracted bad weather. However it is likely that the Orcadian weather a few thousand years back was less stormy and slightly warmer than it is now. But the kind of rocks which the builders of the tombs and whatever may have surrounded them, are the same as those one could pull off the cliff top today.

A story teller today cannot reproduce the kind of talking that must have gone on. Perhaps these people used words which could have several meanings, according to how they were spoken and in what context, as happens in today's African languages, where often key words have several layers of meaning. But assuredly people enjoyed using words and remembering them and stringing them together. Soon it will be time for Pigsie to speak, for he likes using words, even when he has to do it in a whisper.

The sea was chewing away at the cliff far down below. The sun was high among small flimsy clouds, the grass was dry and hot. They had been lifting the flat stones, carrying them on ropes of twisted hide, six men to a stone. You had to be careful. One man had lost his toe when a stone had slipped. Stones are stronger than people. They had brought many stones. Slowly, slowly the wall grew. The cliff was made of rocks on a sharp slant. There were always enough broken off. You could not believe now that in winter the sea would heave itself and come roaring up the cliffs, breaking and tearing. Once or twice there had been someone along on the cliff where it should have been safe, perhaps looking for birds eggs, and that person had been flipped off the cliff like a fly off a wall and no more seen.

Yes, there was danger everywhere. The Moon Woman who pulled the sea, who was not anywhere, who was not a real woman, she made danger, pulling danger and pain out of the air, out of the place of the eagles. Unless one gave her something, a gift, a body. Then at the end she and the great sea birds and perhaps the eagles ate the flesh and the bones were given back and taken over by the Keeper, Sun Man, so that in time the person whose bones they were might live again. It was honourable to become bones and be put carefully into the great bone place and stay there until — well, until. If you became very old or very ill it was good to be aware of the honour coming to you. You could sit on the flat space with the sun-warmed stones and think about this. It was bad to be taken by the sea and the moon. Sometimes a boat with people in it, perhaps fishing with lines for the big fish, would get dragged into the white current; then the sea would have its will of them. That was bad. But now the place of the bones would have one more wall round it, would be safer and better for the bones.

The place itself was made of stones. Inside it was dark, so dark you could only just see the bones, remembering carefully which was your grandfather and which your father, since they must be honoured differently. Grown persons will say what they will want put there when the time comes to honour his or her own white bones, which knife or hammer, which pot, which beads. There was also children old enough to have been named and loved. They would also have things by their small bones, a rush cage with a grass-hopper in it, a whistle, a wooden animal, all for little honourings. And often, almost always, the eagle claws that meant — that meant — but could you put it into words?

Sometimes strangers came to view the bones in their due places, and beyond them the sea, quiet or raging, blue and clear and deep as the eyes of a loved person or sullenly dark. Everyone was proud of the bones. There were other bone places, but theirs was the best. When the men had finished laying the stones of the great wall they would be well fed from someone else's hunting and bread or porridge to go with it. Nor would any man's special woman or wife be likely to refuse a wall builder.

The roof above the bones rose high, each flat stone overlapping a little to reach across and at the top the slab that joined the two sides. All round the heavy dark earth had been packed, rising, rising. It was to keep this from slipping away that a wall must be built. Earth was disobedient; it must be held. People who came from other places, even from across the sea, had never seen so high a built place, but it was not everywhere that you found flat stones like those that made up your own great cliffs where you could see rows on rows of them, set slant as though some great careful hand had done it. It was told that very long ago there had been no Sun Man, only a Moon Woman. She put her mark on young girls. Instead of the Sun Man she had the sea eagles and it was because of that coming together that bodies must be given to the eagles and the Moon Woman before their bones could rest and be honoured. Perhaps this was not so, perhaps it was a story, but if a story is told many times it grows a body. So you must be careful what story you tell.

It was also said that the big bad Moon Woman had once had an honouring place, but somehow it was not at all like their honouring place and it had been pulled apart and scattered by the Sun Man and the bulls. After that came the beginning of their own honouring place where the bones lay and where you must go down on your knees before you could get in. But all that was long, long from now.

One of the young men carrying the stones, whose mother was sister to the man whose toe had been broken by another stone, liked telling stories. He was not always careful. Sometimes they were the stories he had dreamed and it would have been better not to speak them out. He had once had this dream that a fish had come up out of the sea, flapping, and had bitten the foot of his mother's brother and he told it with the kind of words that made his friends laugh. But it would have been better not to have told it, because there came a time when the stone had slipped and broken the bone of his uncle's toe and torn it almost off, and the end of it was that the nasty dangling toe had to be cut off. Of course someone told about the story. Then this uncle was very angry and so was his mother, who beat him with her stick and told him he must now go and carry stones instead of his uncle. And so he did, but when his uncle was walking again he came back to stone carrying, which was an honourable thing, but always made the young man, who was called Pigsie after his pet pig, have the worst bit of carrying. Pigsie had a better name, only nobody called him by it, except sometimes his mother when she was in a good mood. Now stones are never the same all the way round and it is harder to catch on to one bit than to another. So Pigsie had the worst of it over the stone carrying, and both his uncle and his other uncle and his older brother by another mother used to say uncomforting things about him to one another. Naturally it was a family stone carrying, but his other uncle was stupid or perhaps he didn't hear very well.

There were two younger ones: the same grandmother, different grandfathers and the one opposite Pigsie on the lower carrying end was Pigsie's secret friend who used to go into giggles at Pigsie's stories or even at Pigsie making his special face at No-Toe, whose name used to be Hammer and he had to be called that if you spoke to him. Oh, the complications, oh, the shouting! But how else do we live? It would not be happy or sensible for a man or woman always to have the same name over everyone. We have to make room for the spirits. The younger ones had to take the stones that the older ones decided on, even if they knew that there were better stones that anyone in their senses would have chosen. Or so they said. So they would get the hide ropes under the front end of old No-Toe's chosen stone and then jam in bits of stone while the old ones sat on their back ends chewing nice leaves which their women had collected for them. The last heave of the stone lifting was between Pigsie and Giggo his friend and it could be a nasty one if the stone was the least bit unbalanced. Oh, so many near misses! Then off and up to the dyke and the team there handling it on. But they had some strong bits of timber. That wasn't the worst bit. And the dyke grew. The carriers sat back and watched till their stone was well and truly bedded.

There was time to talk and time to remember. Such things had happened which must be brought out and looked at, turned over and over by tongue skills. And look, so many of them are about the bone place which matters to everyone. And about strangers. Yes, there was plenty to remember, mostly pleasantly, about them.

In the light time of year the Stick people would send a message with gifts to say they were coming: meat was brought, young meat. It would be good to see them. Then one day you would hear the voices of shells and the crying and bird noises of stretched strings and along they would come, painted, as many as could be counted on two hands twice over. They carried their big Stick wrapped in lamb skins and fox tails. Stick, stick, come quick. That was what the girls sang and our own girls too. Yes, Pigsie thought, hadn't he caught Ba singing that? So what did she do it for, what?

Then later the Goat people were likely to come. They too sent meat ahead of them and cheese. But sometimes the meat was tough. Pigsie and his friend remembered how hard it was to chew. And a joke they had made about it. There were not so many of them and one or two always had sore eyes. When they grew old they could not see properly. They walked into things. It was funny. But not for them, they were angry but there was nobody to hit. People stopped these old ones from walking into fires or over cliffs, but perhaps one day one of them would not be stopped. Then he would go bounce, bounce down the cliff and the sea would eat him up. When the Goat people came they wanted to see girls, but the girls had a trick of not being there.

Their own visits were good, except that food must be found and sent. The Goat people had a bone place and so had the Stick people, not as good as our own eagle place, but you must praise it, using the right words. There were also the Fish people with the long sand strip and their bone place high up. All their bones must be honoured. Pigsie himself had been on two visits; he had felt proud and excited. His mother had painted him up so that he looked fierce and showed him how to flap his arms like eagles. He had blown loud noises on grass leaves and clicked stones together. He had touched some of the Stick girls, but the one he most wanted to touch had told him he was too young. So he had made up a story in his head about her, a funny story but not good. It made her say angry things, but he — not good, not good. He often told it to himself, but he did not say it aloud, he did not want Giggo his friend to hear it. Perhaps on his next visit? If she was not angry. But what if he had to stay there? And be a Stick. And be painted differently, like they were. How would it be? Good — or not good?

But Giggo was pulling at him to talk, to tell a new story. And the stone they had brought was being shifted by the wall-makers. It would fit better in another place. They measured it with finger-spans; No-Toe argued with them. It was nice to argue about stones. The two old men argued like two bulls. So then?

'There was somebody,' Pigsie whispered to Giggo, 'who had a special honouring stone all chosen out for his bones. That was a great old pounder you could use on anything at all — on anything between two legs. He carried it everywhere, even when he turned into a herd bull, only he had his hands. Ah, that was the best! Even though his front hoof had a bit off.'

And good friend Giggo began to pick it up to make the right faces as the cows names came up and what they were best at. All passing between them out of the corners of the mouth, names like their Aunties names only a bit mixed up, oh clever Pigsie!

Well, in the story when it came to the last of the cows he couldn't quite make it and the cow began to fidget — here Pigsie began to wriggle and make faces — so he took his grinder out and it was the least bit rough so he was polishing it up, but the cow was getting impatient and she grabbed it with her you know what and in it went and his hand after it. Well, that was fine, cow bull, cow bull, and then the chip place on his hoof began to um um — and he had to scratch, so he pulled out his hand and left the honouring stone behind. And there it is to this day. Oh poor cow, poor cow, poor Auntie!

He had to end because the old men were getting to

their feet, proud of the way their stone had set into the wall, chewing away at their bits of brown, salty sea stuff, spitting it around. All wore their sheepskins for work. Now Pigsie was thinking of his story, how he had put his hands onto a bull, how he had punished uncles, oh the things you can do with words! And when he looked across at his friend, there were his mate's lips twitching over a mouthful of laughing.

Well, that was their day, to and fro till they began to smell cooking, and the wall crawling along, butter-milk and praise brought over by the women for the proud stone carriers and builders. If it wasn't laying the great flat stones it was patching in with small stones and every time they went over near the cliff edge, the sea worrying away below, waiting its time. But it was always the old men who got the first go at the buttermilk.

At last the dinner smell was strong and at last the old men said time to stop. No-Toe glared at Pigsie and Giggo, who dutifully told one another that 'the Ham-mer says we can go and eat,' and off they bounced away from the uncles to the houses, the cooking smoke and the girls' voices. Pigsie went to his mother's house and stooped in under the heather roof. His mother said 'Where's the wood for the fire?'

He said I'm hungry. Working all day, stones. Stones for the wall. Ba can get the wood.'

Ba was his sister. His mother scowled at him. 'Ba must stay here. Do the grinding. You boys —— '

Well, he knew that Ba liked going for wood. She liked boys helping her, trying to touch her, well, even getting a nip but maybe giving her small things, a suck of honey, a handful of nice shells or whatever. Soon she would be out of her mother's house. Yes, she was round the corner rubbing away at the grinding stone, cross-looking, the heap of barley meal hardly enough for porridge. True enough there wasn't much wood left, nor much turf. After the storms the men would go down to the hollow place between and behind the cliffs where the waves ran on to the sand at the land edge of the geo. It was here that the sea left wood for the fires, sometimes big wood for roofs or bits of nicely curved hardwood for tools, but mostly cooking wood. It was a hard pull up with a full load and you couldn't blame a girl if she took a helping hand. It was said that if the wood sparkled it was good luck. 'After my porridge I'll get enough for the fire,' he said. 'Promise.'

His mother shook her head. 'Hammer should feed you. If only you hadn't made him angry — you and my mother's daughter's no-good son!'

'He says they've killed the old goat,' said Pigsie. Old goat was tough but if you boiled him down there was good broth. 'Porridge,' he said gloomily, looking into the pot. Still there were eggs in the hot ashes. His younger brothers no doubt. Two of them were chasing about and yelling. He spooned himself out a good dollop of porridge and took two eggs — one was bad. His mother went on muttering. 'Hammer should feed you. You should go to his fire. Why is he still angry?'

Pigsie made a face. He half knew that the old man half knew that he was making up more stories. But all the same he had the right to good food. Meat. Not porridge. 'Still hungry?' his mother said, not very kindly. 'Go there then! Say I sent you.'

He got up. On his way he looked at his sister Ba, short name for a very long one. She was sitting back on her heels from the grinding stone, running her fingers through her hair and yes, smirking at him. Could she —— Those beads were new surely. Well, good luck to her. 'When I've eaten,' he said, 'eaten properly, I'll carry wood.'

'Ha!' said Ba, 'you can do the grinding!' They ended making nasty faces at one another.

He went to Hammer's house. It was bigger but he did not much like the smell. However, Giggo was there already and had a good bone; he was cracking and sucking the end. The old man had taken off his top sheepskin and had his big rough-woven piece over his shoulders and the catch across fastened into the loop. It must be nice to have this, Pigsie thought, but you had to have two women to do it, what with twisting out the threads from the sheeps' wool and dipping them into some women's brew, and one holding on while the other put the threads through and tightened them. And then dipping it again in the special wetting stuff they had. Two wives. But they had to be fed. It must feel nice, a soft woman, two soft women, better than the hard edges of the sheepskins.

He sat down beside Giggo at the far side of the fire. In a bit one of the small girls came across with a couple of ribs. That meant four good mouthfuls and then a nice bit of time chewing. The old man nodded at him from across the fire. Perhaps it was all right now.

He and Giggo had a tiny whisper, nothing that would cross the fire; then it was time to get his mother's wood. He cut across to the head of the geo and the path down to the beach and wondered if Ba had gone too, in spite of his mother. He found some good bits and started dragging them. When he got back there was Ba grinning. Yes, she'd been down too, not that she'd got as much as he had. She only wore a short apron but so many strings of beads, some young girls' worthless berries and feathers and that, but a few good bone beads. He looked cautiously to see if there were bite marks or bruises on her front and back. Yes, he thought, but what about the legs? Suddenly he had a feeling about his sister, so juicy, but stuffed the feeling back. Thought instead about that Stick girl, no, he wasn't too young! Ba didn't seem to be hungry; perhaps she'd been eating elsewhere.

They did some more carrying next day. But the builders wanted smaller stones, so the old men did nothing but sort out the right ones and never did a spot of carrying. Pigsie's elder brother by another mother took over, shouted at them and that was really worse. Nobody else could say a word. Uncles and big brothers were horrid, sisters were nice.

The days when it wasn't their turn Pigsie went out with his sling and enough good stones. It was mostly heather and bushes up at the back, beyond the fields, but he got a wild duck, knocked it over with a sling shot, then pounced and wrung its neck. He saw no deer and this was not the time for the seals to come up into the geo. Sometimes No-Toe sent someone else in his place and then the other uncle was the one who shouted at Pigsie, and was also the one Pigsie made up his stories about after they had brought the stone over to the dyke and were lying back. Sometimes the stories would be about what he and Giggo and the other young ones would do later on when they themselves were the ones to shout and be obeyed and get the best bits of meat. And besides this they could swim in the clouds and ride on swans.

If you worked on the wall you had to pass the place of the bones and there was the keeper of the bones who was older than Hammer. It is frightening to be so old, to live so long. Did he still want a woman? Perhaps everyone was alike to him.

Also the keeper kept track of what was happening

out at the high rock. Were the big birds visiting? Sometimes there might be more than one body there, with branches and light earth over it, waiting to become bones. The smell kept people away, only the keeper was used to it. Also the keeper had charge of what the bodies needed later for their honouring. Yes, Pigsie thought, he must gather in the bones. Yes. When he had taken them back from the high rock and the attention of the sea eagles, the Sun Man and the Moon Woman who came up from the Underneath where she went when you could not see her in the sky.

Pigsie always went a long way round so as not to meet the keeper face to face. It was the same with the others, even his elder brother. The wrong smell? Yes that was it, and the way he looked at you, a measuring look. Or maybe it was all right for old Hammer. It was most likely that old Hammer had already chosen what was to go with his bones at their honouring when the time came to lie down.

The dyke grew slowly, slowly. The day was too long. Then it grew less long. It was berry and nut time. It became clear that Ba had been with someone. There was a time of anger, their mother scolding at Ba and making a lot of switching at her legs.

Then Ba spoke to her mother's elder sister and after that there was much talking. Pigsie was pushed out of the way by the women, only he managed to see that two of his aunties went off one morning, and suddenly he knew where they were going. They stayed away for three nights and Ba cried. But when they came back they had caught a big boy. Pigsie shouted rude things at him, but he was pleased inside. The boy was one of the Sticks who had come to make the visit to the bone place. Ba had pulled him in, clever Ba. He had left his friends to follow the crook of her finger. This was something that only a woman could do. She was bait in the trap for the Stick to fall into. As he himself half wanted to take the bait of that Stick girl. Now some of the boys who had helped Ba with her wood came and said nasty things to the Stick. But they did not mean any harm and the Stick knew that. Pigsie was told by his mother to say good words, the right words, to the Stick and so he did. This was exciting. It was going to be good to have someone new to listen to his stories.

Ba pretended to be very surprised, very frightened. But she was really pleased. Pigsie knew that. She and the Stick were put into a small house of birch branches. Ba had to be pushed in, but after that you could hear them laughing.

Then there were older people coming over and the Stick was taken in front of them and they painted him a little. After that there was grain being steeped and turning into something prickly on the tongue, warm in the belly, so that even the older persons enjoyed touching one another and making jokes, and Ba was called Sprouting Barley. She was pleased with herself and the good stone and turf house that was being built for her. Then days went by and it was time for her to make the big choice.

She was dressed in new lambskins, one of them a tight apron, showing off where there was a new person to come. Then she was being sung off and the Stick boy, who was now to be Pigsie's younger brother, put a woven piece that his mother and her sisters had made, over her shoulders. Now everyone was part of everyone else, standing by while Ba was taken to the keeper of the bones.

Oh, Pigsie was proud of her! She was not afraid. 'Down,' said the keeper, 'down and under,' and then 'to your finding.' All repeated in low voices 'to your finding.' And now Ba was on her hands and knees at the way in, under and between great stones.

She was afraid and also not afraid. The new person inside her stirred, wanting to know. As she got through the narrow place and her eyes began to become accustomed, she knew that here were many spirits but only one that mattered. She was now standing up and there were small cruisies all along and the soft filtered light from the place where she had gone between stones on hands and knees as was necessary. The keeper said nothing. The little cruisies were spots of light on the white bones and their honourings. She was now in some other presence. She moved in it. Fear had left her, she was waiting, almost as she had waited in the soft sand behind that rock in the sun-warmed geo a few moons back.

She heard the voice of the keeper. But whatever words had been used they had gone past her ears into her fingers, her touchers. They moved without her awarenesss, lifted and stretched out and up, past bones untouched, into darkness. At last they touched on bone in the upper shelf without her knowledge. They closed on a stone axe head. She felt the tightening of her fingers on the honouring, streaming out both ways to her and from her. The keeper put a grip on her, firmly and softly, pushing her back, back to the square of light, to the way out into the real world on hands and knees as one must.

There was Pigsie. There was her mother, and her uncles. She looked at them as though they were strangers. And then she looked past them at the young man whom she had seen among the real strangers, who had come down into the geo along a path he had never known and they had sat for a little on the sand without speaking. Then she had told him he must help her to get the driftwood. It had been hard work and then the pulling ache in arms and back stopped and another kind of ache started, a sweet one, a honey feeling, a high summer, a building up and letting go to fall into deep seas, the touching of fish, of newness, of life. She remembered that and it was sweet like remembered honey. That young man was standing beside her mother and he was looking at her. He was new, he was anxious, he was afraid. She was not afraid. She had seen what was needed and she had chosen.

He came close to her now. He whispered: 'What do you hold?' She opened her hand and saw what was in it. It was an old axe head, yes, yes, but whose?'

They all looked to keeper. 'Hammer will ask,' said one of the other uncles, shoving Ba and what she held towards keeper. And Hammer drew a deep breath and asked.

'That is a man's honouring,' said the keeper, 'she will bring us a man.' So, thought Ba, this is what comes of it. 'And the man will be —— ' he pointed at Hammer, 'your father's father's brother! That was his honouring stone. He has slept long. Now he will live again. There!' And he pointed so hard at Ba and her big stomach that she jumped aside with a cry.

Her mother caught her strongly and gently and said 'Yes, yes, that will be good.' And then 'I knew when I had you coming —— '

'What?' asked Ba.

'That you were the hook who would bring back one of the well remembered, a great one. Great on the sea and the land.'

Ba looked down at herself and the swelling under her apron that moved in her. Keeper was saying 'He went far, he found others and spoke with them. He was made welcome. He brought back knowings. Even from across the sea. Went and came back. When he is with us again you will show him his axe head and he will be happy.'

'Yes,' said Ba, 'yes, yes.' Before this she had been more than once to watch how an honouring thing had been shown to a bearing woman, as she was, or else to a small child who had picked it up as if he or she knew it was theirs, and this showed that the spirit had passed. This way there were still and always people. Coming back to be together. It was good. Now for a time even her brother, even Pigsie, would honour her, the carrier. She had brought a new man in from outside and also one of themselves coming back: two persons. Two honours.

But Pigsie was thinking of a funny story about Ba having this baby and out it would come with the axe in its hand and give young Ba a terrible smack and she would throw it into the fire and that would be the end of great-great uncle! No, the one it would smack wouldn't be Ba, poor little Ba swelling up, it would be her man got an axe smack — yes, maybe this axe-baby would come out running and ever so bright red — or bright blue! Oh the funny stories Pigsie had tucked away and couldn't even tell them aloud to his friends! How was it that a lot of them were somehow funny stories about uncles and the things that might happen to them? Did other people have funny stories running through their heads, wanting to come out and be told? Maybe. But Pigsie was going to make a story one day and in that story he himself would — yes, he would — catch that old Moon Woman up there and pull her down so she would eat all those uncles — and then — and then — she would turn into — into what? — into a Stick girl — and then ——

Pigsie became such a good story-teller that he could sit on a rock in the sun wriggling his toes and people would gather round him and squat in the heather, boys and girls mostly, but often enough one of the old ones, and he knew that nobody would tell him to get up and do this or that. Because that would stop the story coming out of his mouth. So he would look at the people he had in his head, behind his eyes, and they would be doing funny things or if they were not doing them they were certainly going to or they had just finished. Sometimes there were girls lying on their backs with their legs loose, laughing and crying, but all of a sudden one of these girls would shoot into the sky like a bird diving but the other way up, up, and she would turn into a — what? Or there would be a strong, strong man who could burrow into the ground and find a beautiful axe and it would jump into his hand and do whatever he wanted — oh there were so many stories.

The man in the stories was always himself but stronger and taller, big like a high hill, blowing fire, sucking up waves full of fish, anything, and the girls were like — like that next time you went to visit the

Sticks and you were not too young and the girls caught you and you had to stay, oh a long time. It was good-good at first, but then you got tired of it and then — but that was a kind of mixed story that he didn't like so much and if he told it, well, it was not like it truly was and that made him sad. So he had to think quickly of a better story. Always there was another story coming up and people asking for it and bringing him things to help him to tell, so that he never wanted for food or drink or a warm place in winter. Yes, they were proud of him; people came from a long way to look and listen. He fathered children. He never had to work. He lived in such a way that he turned into a story himself.

So the years and the generations went by and nothing terrible happened. Sometimes there would be a run of bad seasons and fewer people, but then again there would be a change, more children growing up, more sheep, more goats, more cows. People got to know more about the beasts and also more about crops, why you should pick out good things to eat and help them to grow. The place where the tomb had been built long ago and protected with strong walls was not much changed, though the sea was a little nearer. The eagles still wheeled above the cliffs and people still got together and talked about what happened before they could remember themselves, because there had to be a strong tie, a rope to hold onto between then and now.

And now I must come into the story myself, because I have made an assumption that may be wrong but, after all, it just might be right. I assume something which I have already hinted at: that there could have been some other rather different people somewhere in the complicated land area of Orcadia, where there are so many separate islands and partly cut off peninsulas, cliffs and bogs, places where the sea has wriggled in as though it wanted to break through into fresh water. There have been changes in the sea's reach along the beaches and edges, which could have wiped out the evidence of any people who might have lived there. For most people lived near the sea, the great provider.

So there were the Eagle people, talking and playing games, quarrelling and laughing and saying loud things which they want others to hear. In some years Keeper was important and got the best of everything, but sometimes other people were more important, most of all if they had managed to live for a long time, without illness or accidents, even perhaps to see their grandchildren. These old ones would know what should be done if there were questions. It was important that there should be many questions from the young ones so that they could be told what they must do.

Sometimes for one evening after another in the long light summer there was telling of stories. The stories grew as people thought of more ways of decorating them or of making the right noises to go with them. Here, for instance, was Third-boy, and his father was telling him a story: one that had been told many times.

'Once upon a time,' Third-boy's father began to tell his son,' there was our own storyteller — some say he was hatched in an eagle's nest — and he surpassed all other story tellers. Listen and I will tell you about him.'

'There have always been storytellers. We cannot live without stories. Long, long ago, when these old stones were new, there was a contest of storytellers. It was the old men with beards who set up this contest, but they were still strong enough to tell stories from one sun-setting to the next sun-setting. Yes, truly.'

And here Third-boy's father told his son what kind of stories they were, what animals came into them, what extraordinary things the sea brought into them, how the stories hopped from year to year, always finding something new. Some storytellers were worn out with telling, but three were left: one from the Stick People, one from the Fish People and one from ourselves, the Eagle People. He was of course the best of them and won the prize. Yes, he was the greatest story teller. Everything was given to him. He had only to ask and so it was. He went to the Stick People but came back. Yes, he belonged to us. We are all the children of his stories.'

And so it went on, but Third-boy wanted to know what the prize was.

His father looked round and made a face like a fox and said 'Girls. Girls. And the drink that is made with berries, better than meat.'

'I like meat best,' said Third-boy and in his mind there was a picture of meat laid on the ashes and the juice running and the smell of it catching at one's tongue, one's throat, one's belly. If I had been a story teller Third-boy said to himself, I would make a story about meat.

Sometimes days and days went by and there were only shells or small fish and roots and leaves: times when there was little milk and only the seed corn which must not be touched. You hope someone will kill one of the sheep, even an old, lean one and there would be something to chew. But if there was a sheep killed, Third-boy was not one of those likely to get a good bit. Not yet. One day? Well, perhaps.

In the last two years there had been coming together and talking by the older men and women. They must decide about the field where there had always been barley —— 'Always?' asked one of the women, and there was a prickly feeling, but in the end that was left. It was becoming clear that the corn was not as good as it had once been. The older people talked of strong stalks and heavy heads. But not so now. There was much talking but at long last it was decided that another piece of ground must be made ready for the new crop. This bit of land was further out, sloping towards a hollow, but the grass looked good and so would the corn look. There were too many stones, but if everyone worked, taking away the stones, throwing them into the hollow, digging and turning all together, with foot ploughs or even with a kind of plough which could be pulled by two men, but it was hard, hurting work and why was it always Third-boy who was shouted at to go to the field? Work, work, too much work. When would it end?

Third-boy came back, staggering, breathless, with the skinned meat still dripping down his back. He slung it off onto the flat stone and shouted. The others had smelled it, everyone came running. Big mother had already grabbed three of the young ones and pushed them off to get sticks, more, more, to hurry the fire, oh meat, meat! It was days since there had been meat on the flat stone, so many days. You are tired of porridge and bannocks even with milk and there is not always milk; you are hungry for other things. Sometimes the sea has things to give, but small things. Little rock fish and shells can be thrown into the pot or leaf wrapped into the ashes, but meat must be done right.

Certainly bits and scraps can be pulled or hacked off, stuck on sticks over the flames for a quick treat, but the big piece, oh the big piece, hind legs and back, it must go in the trough with the fizzing stones from the fire hotting the water which is half from the sea, the life juice of the meat reddening it. You lift the fizzing stones from the hottest part of the fire with forked branches and run with them to the trough. There is a pile of fizzing stones. When they cool down you put your hand in warm and pull out the stones to go back to the fire; you lick your fingers and the wet begins to taste. Oh the trough, the trough, finding the right, flat stones, fitting them together tight, tight, joining them with clay, arguing, carrying, days and days! Now it is over. The water gets hot, hot, too hot for your hand; it breathes out and then the little bubbles come and the meat shifts about because the water is alive round it. You must keep on putting in the fizzing stones and the meat will turn from red to brown, and it will be soft to eat when you cut with your knife, soft and warm so your teeth sink in and you feel good all over.

But before this Third-boy has done the proper thing. He has taken out the liver and kidneys, fern-wrapped them and put them in his bag to take over to the old ones who, while their soft and special meat cooks quickly on the ashes of their fire, will in return say over him wise and difficult words. These should be a powerful help to him, but who knows how? Yet he will need help. He knows that. Because of what he has done.

Now Third-boy was the big one, though he would do best to keep his small, unboasting name so that he would not be looked at too much. When First-boy had become hot and hurting and then cold and had been taken to the high cliff of the eagles, and after that gone to the dark, to the Name we do not say, he might have asked to take First-boy's name, but he knew without being told, that it was better not. Names are powerful, they drag at people who own them, they are like stubborn cattle. It was the same with Second-boy's name: you did not think it. But now, even with his small name, the girls came with soft moss to clean the blood off him because it was beginning to smell. Then, when he was clean, two of them went on to rub their own softness against him, nicer than the moss. He need not be small for them. What would he do?

He thought he would tell them, very slowly in big words, how he had walked for a long way, because he was a little angry; he did not want to be told by the old men that the new field must be dug. Then he had seen the deer far off and followed, so carefully, hiding and then running, and then he had thrown his spear and he would tell them what had come in his mind as he watched it strike. He would tell how the deer had sprung and fallen over and how he had raced and leapt to get it before it could struggle up. Oh yes, and the girls would look at him with big eyes, they would make woman noises, they would roll on the ground. And then? Then he would stand and consider and then — then he would pounce as though to kill, but not to kill. Yes, he had brought meat. He smelled it cooking. And everyone had been so hungry.

But could he tell about the — Other? Yes, he must tell because of what he had done. And must undo. If he could. The girls had stopped rubbing against him. They were waiting now for him to tell. And pounce. But no, he could not tell them, he could not pounce on them, instead he had to — not have done what he did. He jumped up, at least he was clean now. He went back to the old ones, where they sat in the open, noble space, their backs to the great bone-house, their faces to the sea. They were eating what he had brought, they looked up, they welcomed him.

Now he was trying to ask, to find out what he should do. He stood among the sitting old ones, some of whom listened while they chewed. Two of them were playing their game with the black and white stones and did not listen, even a little, but the rest wanted to hear something new. He told how he had been out hunting all the long day, away beyond the fields. There had been so much to do in the busy days, digging ditches, clearing stones off the new field, building up those stones into walls, cutting the spiky heads of the bere barley and carrying it in, shouting at the small children, oh everything, herding the cows and the sheep, at the end you had to get away — yes, yes, said the old men, but we have all worked so as to live. So then?

Then at last he had got away into the outside, and he had seen the deer grazing and crept up, quietly, quietly, and thrown his spear. And then he had run to finish it off and then it was on the ground and he had started with his knife. But while he was cutting it up to take back and getting out the liver — for you, as is right — this Other had run against him yelling, screaming. He had seemed to speak words but they were not real words and this Other was smaller than he was, but he had a knife, might have cut, so he knocked him down and hit him with a stone and he lay still. His knife jumped out of his hand before it hurt me.

One of the old men said 'Did you kill him?' It was not clear from his voice whether the answer should be yes or no.

'He might die,' Third-boy said. He had begun not to know.

An old man got to his feet and pulled at one of the two old women. Women did not often grow to be old. But this one had a big skin bag with patterns on it made of shell beads, patterns to keep the things inside safe and powerful. 'Come,' they said. Now he wished he had waited. He could smell the meat cooking, it might be almost ready and surely he himself must eat his fill — he had only snatched a small bit of it scorched over the fire! But no, said the old ones and how they said it frightened him.

They walked past the fields where the beasts were now. It had been day after day with the digging sticks and then it would be day after day again. And in winter you must look after the cows and the sheep: work, work. First-boy hadn't seemed to mind work and besides he had got another name; they had called him Uptop because of that tree he was always climbing. So how was he now, down in the dark, after the eagles, nothing but bones? Or were the bones really him? First-boy used to sing when they were out digging. Second-boy was more of a shirker but he had liked climbing on the cliffs, not just in trees. And then that thing happened; there had been a rattle of stones and just one shout. So he was not even bones. But now they were with the nameless. Where only the moon —— If they were anywhere.

They walked quickly, even the old woman. Perhaps they had been sitting so long they were tired of it as perhaps the dead grow tired of lying. Third-boy led along the hillside, remembering exactly how he had gone, watching for anything to eat, even a big bird, remembering every ragged bush, every stone. It was a long way and the old ones began to be angry and to call him bad names. He would have carried her bag for the old woman but she slapped his hand. But at last they came to the place and the blood and the mess of the cut up deer and the bow of the Other which he had broken because he was so angry, but he had not told them that, and then what he feared, what he wanted undone, the Other lying as he had left him, sprawled, his hands seeming to clutch at grass tufts. He looked younger than he remembered when they were shouting at one another. 'Did I — send him?' Third-boy asked and his voice sounded to him not like his own voice and he was frightened. He wanted to run but his legs shook. The old woman was squatting in the tufts of grass; she put her hands under the shut-eyed head, mucky with blood and earth from the stone. She shifted the head a little and suddenly it was sick, vomit came out of it and then a groaning noise and suddenly it was a person and there in the heather was his knife which Third-boy had knocked out of his hand. It all came together.

The old woman shuffled in her bag and pulled out a chipped little clay pot. 'Water,' she said to Third-boy. He went quickly. It was more like a wet streak on the slope, not bubbling water, but there was a little hollow he could dip into and he tore up long handgrips of wet, cold moss as well.

The old woman worked away and the Other began to mutter, but not real words. The two old ones seemed to understand and looked at one another. They stood over the Other and began to make noises, but these too were not words. So, thought Third-boy, I have not sent the Other to the eagles and the dark and that is good, because if a person sends another then he in turn will be sent. Not by a person but by whatever chooses to do the thing: a cliff, a wave, an illness, even the knowledge that it is happening and cannot be stopped. There is no harm in shouting, even angry words, no harm in drumming by someone's sleep place, scaring his children or pulling off his wife's apron. All this can be undone and a person's friends will see to it that this happens, even if it means giving good things and speaking sweet words. But if a person sends another person into the dark, it cannot be undone. So when the Other sat up a little, leaning against the old woman and made a hating face at him, at least Third-boy knew it could all be made right. Somehow.

The old man picked up the broken bow and seemed to be speaking words; he seemed to be telling the Other that this was nothing, there would soon be another better, stronger bow for him. And then they turned and shouted bad words at Third-boy while he stood trying not to hear. The words fell on him like hail and he felt hurt inside and said to himself that the old ones had eaten his meat and it was hard that the taste had not stayed with them. And yet he was pleased that the Other was living and perhaps was being glad of the hard words.

So now the Other looked more like a person and grinned at him as if after all he had got the best of it. His head was on the old woman's lap. The old man had covered the vomit and blood with heather roots. Third-boy saw he had broken one of the Other's teeth. That was bad. You cannot mend teeth. By now the Other looked like anyone, but his eyes were a funny colour and his hair grew a little differently. And it seemed he could not talk real words. Not to talk is being like a dog. But as he was standing and thinking this and looking down at the Other, the old man came over and shook him and said 'Say this.' And he whispered a noise and pushed him nearer the Other. Third-boy did not want to make the noise, but the old man shook him: 'Say it. No, louder.'

So he said it and the Other's face twitched a little, and now the old man made Third-boy say noises, and it seemed to him that he was somehow speaking, but what he said was not his own but the noises the old man put into his mouth. So what had he been saying? The old woman laughed deep in her throat and told him that he had called the head on her knee brother and after that he had said he would make a new bow and they would eat and all would be well. And the head had said yes, all would be well and called him brother. 'That is a good word,' said the old man. 'Now say it again.'

No, he would not. It was stupid to make these sounds. Like an animal. 'I only say words,' he said, and he made the proud face of someone who says real words. The two old ones were scolding at him; he did not like this. 'But I will do a good thing,' he said, and he went over to what he had noticed almost before he saw the Other lying, and picked up the knife. It was a good knife, the flint even not notched. He held it up for the old ones to see. The Other saw it too; his eyes followed it. Third-boy put it down beside the Other's hand and the Other made that noise that they said was brother. Well, perhaps he would try it.

There was then a kind of game: knife and the noise that said knife from the Other. Man. Woman. Hand. Foot. Water. Some noises were like real words, some were very different, just silly sounds. But the Other became tired, he would not try to stand, his eyes began to shut. Third-boy was fidgeting: how to get back? The shadows were sloping, it would be cold. And there was the deer carcase half cut up, beginning to smell. If only they had fire! 'Fool' said the old man and put his hard forefinger into the small bag on his belt, fished something out, blew on it and a little smoke came trickling out. 'Fire' said the old man and quickly, quickly, Third-boy started to grab bits of dry grass, little sticks, anything — and the fire started. Oh fire, food, life. They toasted small bits cut from the deer on the flames, the fat dripping. But the Other would not eat. He slept. They all slept. There were four persons. That was good.

Back where they came from there was good sleeping and the sea noise gentle. People sleep well with fullness inside them. They wake, happy to be warm, to remember eating. The sun is up and everyone is moving. The children are playing games, throwing things, scratching themselves; they too have eaten meat. You feed the fires and look to see if there are any scraps left. The children are picking over the bones. Be careful how you break the big marrow bones, we need more needles. Yes, there is a sharp bit. If only Third-boy had brought back the whole of the deer! But where can he be? You ask the big girls but they giggle and say he ran away from them. But the old ones, where they sit in the open space where the flat stones get warm in the sun, their back to the great, honoured, bone-place, they tell you, but, like always, they only tell you a little. It seems that Third-boy may have done the bad thing. The worst. He may have sent another person to the eagles. But what person, we are all here? The answer is that it was not one of us, but an Other. So what is that truly? Are there Others? Yes, the old ones say, they live at the far, far edge, it is their sea beyond. They have been there forever. They do not eat bread. Poor things, you say, no bread!

Ah, says the old man, waggling his beard. 'They have porridge, not so good as our porridge. Not always porridge, no.' The old man shakes his head. 'They have poor, small fields, not like ours. We have the best fields.'

The younger men look at one another and screw up

their faces. It is hard work making good fields. The old man goes on: 'We showed them.' A child asks 'What, you?' 'No, no, our fathers' fathers perhaps. It is told. Those Others did not know about fields. Instead they ate deer meat, sea things, roots, leaves. Long ago they had no corn, no sheep, no cows, not a drop of milk.'

'No milk — Oh poor things! The women are sorry for the Others. But some of the men are feeling stronger, better than these Others. Here we have more things, we are glad of them.' But the old man goes on: 'Yes, they are poor things. We showed them. Some came bringing deer meat. They came in skin boats round the edges. Not good boats like ours. We gave them — yes, lambs. To the Others. They had no word for lambs. So we gave them the word. The word and the lambs.' The old man looks pleased, thinking of this. 'Yes, it is good to give. Then you are the top one, giving. Later we gave calves.'

Another of the old ones, a woman, clicks two stones, she wants to speak. 'We gave. But they are clever, they have good skins. Deer skins. They put roofs of skins on their houses and the skins have red and blue on them. Patterns. Learn to speak their way, you might get one. They hunt, they are clever with bows, they make traps, they speak to birds, they know all the roots, all the berries, all the things from the sea. Their pots are full.'

A man says: 'But their women are small and tough. They do not smell good like our women.' He looks round, hoping that some woman is listening. Someone laughs and asks how he knows. He scowls, mutters. Perhaps he has never smelled even one woman of the Others. All the same he is right, we are better. We know that. But we did not truly know that till now. For now we know that the Others are real.

A still older old one looks up, scratches his beard, spits. He will tell us more. That is what the old ones are for, to tell us more about everything. This knowing is inside them. That is why, when they are sent to the eagles, they do not altogether go. They are not only bones in darkness. We hear them still. We can ask them by name and we are told, perhaps in words, perhaps not. We ask through Keeper who is able to wake them, but not always. This old one will tell us in words because he is still waiting for the eagles, still in the sun. He knows. We are quiet. We listen. He says that the Others herd the deer, almost like cows. They and the deer came together, long, long ago. They speak to the deer. That is why this Other whom you will see, was so angry. They speak to the deer before killing it. The deer must allow them to kill it. He shakes his head. It is a strange thing.

A child asks: 'But are they persons? Like us?' The old man laughs and says 'You will see.' So now everyone is talking about this amazing thing that has happened and the sun is moving across, making the sea blue, and most of the children have gone round and down to see if there is anything nice for them caught among the stones on the beach. We still have some driftwood, but the fires are always hungry. They must also bring wood. Someone has porridge making in a pot among the ashes. No, more than one.

And then, who comes? One of the children runs, jumps in, says it is the two Old Ones and Third-boy, who has yet more meat! Quick then, the fizzy stones, we eat again! But there is a person with him, someone we have never seen, it must be the Other. So Third-boy did not send him to the eagles, we shall all see the Other. This is a day that will be talked about.

Four persons come. The Old Ones are tired, are a

little angry, do not want to be asked questions. And Third-boy says 'this is my new brother.' But not First-boy, not Second-boy, not any more. New. So someone scoops out thick porridge from the pot, putting it onto flat shells, first for the Old Ones, then for Third-boy and his new brother. Milk is brought. But this brother puts his finger into the hot porridge and licks it and shakes his head, makes a stupid face. He does not like the taste of our porridge, it must be different from theirs. But it must certainly be better. He is stupid not to like it. And we hear that the Others have no bread. But today we ourselves have no bread. We ate all there was, eating it with the meat. How good it was! But nobody has made any more. Not this day. Nobody has been grinding. Lazy women! Lazy girls! They have been eating meat, not grinding. They should be beaten. But there is meat again, Third-boy is coming, he is bringing it.

Oh look, the meat, the meat again, we shall get fat! The fizzy stones go in and the water heats up. There is not so much on the front legs and back, but yes, it will do, we shall all eat, look, the bubbles are coming. And there will be the shoulder bones, so good for digging. With a shoulder blade, if you say the right words to it, you can dig in the sand, quick, quick, and get the juicy beast that lives at the end of the long shells. The neck bones will be right to thread and rattle.

There is the Other coming slowly. He sits with us. Who will touch him? His eyes are a little different. Perhaps his hair. Third-boy sits down beside the Other, he says words but he also says not-words. We are sorry for this Other. We have more things. Our women smell better. And we have our great strong bone place where those who are sent go and are safe. Keeper looks after them. Do the Others have a bone place? Perhaps. We must ask. But who dares? So, will the Other stay with us? It might be good, he might be lucky. But we are a little frightened. You never know. The big girls are prowling round, one of them sits beside the Other, how brave she is! She is touching him and perhaps he will answer, perhaps she will be able to tell us all what he is like.

So now there are two good days with food to eat, meat and marrow bones, good dreams. Summer and sun is the best time for dreaming and eating. But then the sun becomes tired, goes away earlier. Winter is the worst time. In winter Third-boy must go out in the few hours of light, searching for food. The sea is the best provider; there are almost always low-tide shells, even if the best of the near limpets have been knocked off. The brown tangle comes in and at least helps the sheep and cattle beasts, those that were not killed off in autumn and salted; that meat is not the best of eating. Sometimes there are dead, battered fish; winter is no time to take the boats out. The land gives little, only a few roots here and there. Best if you happen on a hoard of nuts left by the four-footed small ones, good eating themselves but not enough to share. In winter death comes nearer; the bodies are light. Next summer there will be fewer old ones with their stories, fewer small children. Sleep long in winter if you can, if you are sure of waking at the end.

But there was another deer killed. It was thought that the Other had called it. But that was not easy to ask. So now strips of meat have been salted and smoked, to chew on. The Other has stayed with them — his small skin boat has been carried to a safe place. He has learned to like bread and there is one woman who likes to bake it for him. But he is frightened by the big songs when everyone sits swaying, and by the thought of the great Bone Place. But, Third-boy tells him, the singing is to bring the sun back, the light, the warmth. How? Third-boy does not know. The keeper knows; that is why we feed him first. But there is also a certain woman who eats; food is brought to her. But it is not clear to me why: not yet. Perhaps one day. But I have heard it is about the moon. Women know the moon and the moon knows the sea. Perhaps my mother half knew, but she is dead. The old ones know but they do not tell.

But the dark time goes on. The singing goes on. And the Other thinks, not in the words he has learned from Third-boy and also from two or three of the girls, but in his own words, which he can sound to himself, of certain things that he knows must be done in the dark time to make it end. So will these people do these things. Or is there another secret?

Then at last the sun is beginning to warm up the ground, to bring life back. Now the Other makes pictures in his mind of his own place. He thinks about his boat; it has been pulled up safely. But he must go and look at it, must try to tell his new brother Third-boy what he wants. When the good, calm days come back, the two of them begin their journey, carrying flats of bread for a gift. They cross from one small, sheltered bay to another, which they can see. There are people in this other bit of land. Sometimes they see one another; they can throw words back and forth. A long time ago Third-boy's mother's mother came from there. They had a bone place, songs; they were real people.

The skin boat is not too heavy. The Other had carried it alone when he came, looking for a fat deer to speak to and then, when it was allowed, kill. Now the Other carried the paddle; he does not let Third-boy try it. They cross to yet another land with sheep, but though they smell smoke they do not go near. After that comes one more crossing. In all these places are shells and leaves or roots to eat. But after that there comes a long, hungry walk, seeing not one person nor yet sheep or cows or goats, during the whole day. They cross hills and push through rocks and thickets and brambles and find a way round the edges of dark, hungry bogs.

And now they are near. The Other begins to dance a little. It all starts to happen. Third-boy has learned from the Other to say a few good things in their words. He is a little afraid but not for long. He finds that what has been said about the smell of their women is not true. No, it is a good smell. There are not many of them, perhaps three hands only, but they are all persons, men, women and little ones. And so. And so.

We leave them and go on. It seems likely that, once you get a real mixing of people, the smaller languages and cultures die out or are kept for special occasions. Words may be spoken only by women or survive in rhymes and place names, fears or hopes no longer taken seriously. Gradually there will be contact and exchange, all through the Orkney mainland, though the smaller islands might still be partly cut off, only connecting when tides or currents are favourable.

The years and centuries go by, the births and deaths. Slowly changes come in people's lives, a new way of decorating pots, of making better knives and adzes, scrapers and axes, of building stronger boats, of fitting new words to old tunes. All ways of thought and imagining about what you cannot understand, whether or not you name them in religious words, last for a time and then wear out. If they appear again, for better or worse, they are different. Perhaps that happened in the place at the top of the cliffs where the little group of elders used to sit close to the great tomb and be as one with their ancestors inside it.

While changes came so slowly in Orcadia or Scotland itself, in the easier, warmer parts of the world records were being kept, for some kinds of writing had started; much was known and passed down about crops and animals and weather, about counting and measuring, about building and decorating, the metals and the clays, about silk and cotton and also about the stars, the sun and the moon, and about the averting of the many kinds of disaster which befall humans. There was war and there was poetry. Above all there was exchange, both of things and ideas. In some places this had already turned into trade, but less so in the further places where gifts were not bought but admired and exchanged.

Down the centuries it becomes easier to get from one place in the world to the next, either for people or things passed from hand to hand. There would be the beginnings of trackways through forests, round the edges of hills or lakes, across difficult rivers and between mountain ranges. It would be strange if there had been no more new families crossing to the Orkneys, settling there, building and digging and getting in touch with their neighbours. Sometimes things would go wrong, a whole group might die out, perhaps of an epidemic or perhaps in a hungry year. No doubt there were quarrels, but there is no evidence of anything like today's hatred and attempted annihilation of the enemy, even down to his thoughts and loves. The cycle of the tides did not alter, nor yet the seasons of natural growth, and people adapted to them in their various ways, under sun, moon and stars.

It is likely enough that one group of people had better luck and the ability to use it. If the geology was right, your luck was in. Other things followed if you wanted them to follow. It does not need a war leader or a high priest, but if someone seems to be lucky, as Hands was in his day, others want to follow, to be close, to share a little of the luck. In return they will work, give things, hunt and fish and plough with and for the lucky one, and hope for protection, for the strong warm house with food and drink for all.

The lucky one is probably a man, but may be a woman. The evidence of the bones looks like that. On the main Orkney island there was such a man. He had been a strong child; his mother had fed him well. He had keen eyes and ears. When he was grown, he and his friends sailed over to the big land beyond and there killed wolves and bears and big deer and wild cattle with enormous horns. It is said that he also killed a great beast with sharp claws and wings and two roaring heads. When he came back the boat was heavy loaded. There were great bundles of skins and salted meat and bags of honey comb, but also beautiful and exciting things from far off beyond the sun's path: woven stuff, smooth and soft, shining beads, polished black rings, as well as a thing which he hung by a cord on his own neck; this was a serpent's egg that always shone with a yellow sun-born brightness. There was another sun-bright thing, round, a hand's breadth, with marks that meant it was itself a small sun. Sometimes this lucky man held it on his knee and looked at it for a long time. This was good, but the best was a long knife with a new kind of blade, a beautiful feel and colour. You could slice the head off a sheep with one sweep of it. He had two axe heads of the stuff and a few smaller knives which he gave to his best friends. Only the sun things he always kept close to himself. By now it had been borne into him that he and the sun were somehow one thing.

People came to look at him and his treasures. Heads of small groups needed to be recognised, spoken to, urged to accept gifts. He fed them and gave them sleeping space. Many brought him meat and corn, for he had many mouths to feed. In this way he would speak to them and they would tell others what he had said, what he looked like and how his house looked and who were his best friends. He kept the great fears away, the fear of darkness and with it the fear that one day the sun would refuse to rise and the chill, shadow-making moon would take over the world.

He was a generous man, not one to remember a quarrel; he in turn respected the old and wise. When beautiful girls came his way he did not refuse them. The old ones spoke to him on matters of life and death, sun and moon. He respected the moon woman, who had been his mother's friend and had given him a lucky birth. He understood that the tides were under the orders of the moon. The moon woman and certain of the old men had spoken to him about time and how to divide it and put a yoke on it, how to know ahead the strange dances of the stars. They had made drawings in the sand.

There came a year when he had brought in many men after harvest and gave them drink to make them bold and tongue-loose, so that all could talk over what would have to be done so as to take hold of sun and moon and be done with some kinds of fear. All went well. There was agreement. But then came a sudden new sickness, striking here or there, and in spite of her knowledge and position their moon woman herself was stricken by this sickness and died. How could that have happened? People looked up at the night sky and wondered and shivered. Was the moon in its right place? How were the tides? What could happen? What will the sun man do to help us?

Those who called themselves the eagle people, they lived across the water on the far side. They did not know about this man with the sun things. And then he stretched out his hand. Then new things began to happen.

Where had the men gone? Well, everybody that mattered knew and those who did not matter were given jokey answers. Some women complained, but they were looked down on by the others who had been told and felt themselves enlarged, in touch with great things. It was also said that when all was ready they too would go in a boat or, perhaps better, it would be men from that place, wherever it was, who would come to them. That would be good. New men who would make strong children.

Men think more of what they are going to do. They like to boast about this, to make up stories. The women make stories, too, but they are often about things that the men have forgotten already, bad winters, children that have died, or about when they were young and had been given presents and choices, and work had not been so hard. Sometimes women half remembered long ago, when the Stick men or the Big Fish men came and how well they were painted and the Big Fish men brought necklaces of fish bones and some of them stayed. That had been good. But you have to watch the Fish children because they run out into the big waves and are carried away to be made to work for the Big Fish under the water, and never come back.

The women's boat was usually crewed by girl children of the Big Fish men; they did not go out so far as the men's boats, but they called to the fish and did well enough. Their boat had a mast and a sail made from several calf skins sewn together. It was not painted with an eagle as the men's sail was, but with a round kind of thing. Only some of them knew what to call it.

Half the time now there would be two or three women talking about why and where the strongest men had gone in that other boat as far as you could see, and then further still. It had started when the two men from outside had come and made promises. There had been great talking and presents given. It would be something to remember for always. Those men had been honourable and important. They had beautiful shining stones and the teeth of many beasts slung round their necks. Their own men would come back some day with such things.

Those who knew where their men had gone and to do what, were anxious, but also proud. They asked one another why it had become necessary to measure and tie down time. In case it stopped? No more harvest, no more night and day! If the sun rolled away and was lost — drowned. Could this happen? Would knowing about it stop it? Would what the men were doing — what they thought the men were doing — make bad things not happen?

We know the moon better, the women said. The Moon Woman herself knew it best and she was not unacquainted with the brother movements of the sun and how both of them, in the time they are not with us, light up the Other Place which was full of what had been people. So full! So large a place, with no edges, no end, so many old ones, so many little un-named ones, so much sadness. The old bones stayed, but the new bones wanted to live. That was a thing they must never do; yet one wanted to pleasure them, to honour them, and also to stop them from coming to live in people's dreams.

This was what the Moon Woman, working with or without Keeper, with or without the younger one who would be able to take her place if — when — it became needful, had to make sure of. On a night of full moon she and Keeper had moved the old bones, which no longer wanted to live again, and put stones over them. But also these bones were given eagle claws in case somehow, some time, they began to grow flesh. Beyond that and most importantly, she had to make sure that the moon was pulling the water for the tides. Sometimes the moon half forgot. Then Moon Woman must face the rising and speak the right words.

By now Moon Woman had allowed a younger woman, whom she had chosen, to learn everything, even the knowledge that was frightening, that hurt. She saw to it that this knowledge was now deep in her follower, so that nothing could shake it. When this younger woman took a man he could not share in this knowledge, any more than her own man had shared. Sharing between man and woman was about other things. She had given her follower a secret name, just as she had been given one, but never spoke it. It was totally shut in. It could not even be spoken in a dream.

The Moon Woman had terrible dreams sometimes, mostly after what she had to do at night. She wanted back her man who had died, but not in the dream shapes he came back in, him turning into something horrible. What had gone wrong, why did he want to frighten her? His bones had been properly dealt with.

He had never been bad to her while he was alive; they had been warm and kind together, had made children. He had never asked her questions which she must not answer. Sometimes she wanted to hurt the women who still had their man or those whose men had gone, but they knew where. Men who would come back. Some of the women said their men came back at night; that might be good-good, but sometimes not. They were dream men, not the real ones who had gone in the boat.

Sometimes Keeper came and nagged at the women; he was getting old. There was a new Keeper chosen, but he had not yet been shown everything. Old Keeper did not want to show him, but he must; he had a pain in his throat, he could not chew properly, when he knocked into a stone he did not heal well. He got angry and then everybody went away and left him. He was angry about most things and especially that fewer people came from Outside to visit the tomb and wait for him to tell them whose bones were where and what was the right honouring of the bones. There had been a time when it was thought lucky for a young woman to go with Keeper, but none of them wanted to do that now. They said he smelled bad. They would rather have the young Keeper, though he did not know so much about the bones.

And then one day, when the sea at the side was smooth and friendly, two of the young ones who were herding the sheep saw a boat coming from the far edge. They rushed back shouting. Everyone came running, Moon Woman among them. She was glad it was her child who shouted loudest; he must be growing strong. Keeper stayed where he was. Perhaps the people in the boat had come to visit the tomb and he must be there. Perhaps they would leave gifts. Such things had been. But Keeper was wrong. In the boat was one of their own men and two strangers. Their own man now had a necklace of bones, all colours, and clay beads, red and black; he had been eating well, you could see that. Everyone waited to be told what would happen.

Then their own man whispered to one of the strangers and pointed. And then both the strangers pointed at Moon Woman, and their own man said 'She must come with us.' She shook her head. Most of the people who had come running shook their heads. No, no, Moon Woman was theirs. She was not to go away.

Their own man said: 'She must come. For a time. Only for a time. We need her. There.' He pointed across the sea. A man came up from the boat. He was mostly wearing yellow earth paint, but he had a shining stone slung round his neck. He brought a big piece of meat and between his hands a great pot filled with corn. He laid these things on the ground. It was the time of year before harvest and they were running short of grain. The pot had marks different from their pots, a thicker rim. They looked at the food and looked away. One or two licked their lips.

Then the yellow-man, the stranger, came nearer. He stood in front of Moon Woman, he took her hand. It went lax in his, she did not know how to speak. Strange hand. If she had been a girl, a wanting girl, she would have known. But not now. She shook her head.

The man spoke. At first it was hard to hear words, real words. Then it became clear that it was only that he did not say words the right way; his words went down his throat. Some were real words, but some said nothing. In a little she was able to listen and understand. His words said that the Moon Woman over there had died before she could work out a certain thing. It was a thing she had to tell them, a true thing. That Moon Woman was old; she had always been there, nobody thought she would die. But there was something they had to get right, had to be told, because they must know about time to come. Because this one was a Moon Woman she could help them. So, the man seemed to say, we need you. To show us. To help us to live.

She looked down at the hand, up at the face. Was he speaking true? For a moment he looked like her own man, kind, asking her for something she could give. She looked beyond him. There was her son who had seen the boat coming. Not her first son, but the one who had lived. Because she had asked the moon for help. At the right time. So was this again the right time to help? She looked at the man and smiled a little. He took the beautiful polished stone into which one could almost see, pulled the cord over his head and put it onto her. So all became clear. She put her hand over it and it shaped itself into her fingers. She said very low: 'I will come.'

And then — then each of the stranger men took one of her hands and all three walked down to the boat as one walks in a dream. She smiled at her son as she passed him. He had been part of a good thing.

While Moon Woman was going slowly to the boat, the man who was one of themselves had found his woman and they had gone together behind a rock. How strange and fat he was! She stroked him, she felt good. In his pouch he had a piece of cooked meat; they ate it together. But he had to go, he was called. Now she knew he was not dead. None of their own men were dead, not one. They had good food.

Moon Woman went down off the grass onto the

sand. She was clumsy getting into the boat, she was not one of the Big Fish children; she had not been in a boat for a long time. She sat with her back to where they were going and she saw everything she knew get smaller so that she could no longer see her son's face. Instead she looked at the two men, wondering if they were truly persons, trying to smell them, but only getting the smell of the sea. She looked also at their own man; she knew what he had been doing with his woman. It was right.

There were four other men in the boat, but it was clear to her that they were not important. They must paddle the boat with strong, hard strokes, while one of the big painted men, as she thought of them now, took the steering oar and the other sat looking at her. This man who was, she thought now, a real person, wanted to tell her things. But for a long time Moon Woman did not listen. She was looking down into the sea. She was aware of huge cliffs, but she did not want to see them. There was a small sail on the boat; it helped with the paddling. It seemed to her to be made not of skins but of something harder and coloured.

And then in a while the stranger turned her, made her look a new way, not at her own place, but at his, for it was coming nearer and nearer. And it made her cry out softly because of something too strange to understand. On the ridge of the land there was something that could not be, standing against the sky, tall and dark grey. Many of them. Taller than two men. Than three men. She could not want to look. And it was late in the day.

This was the time when the moon was clouded by the big shadow which was, somehow, the sun's doing, the bite of jealousy. She would rise late in the night, would dawdle into the day, becoming fainter. At last would be, for a time, lost. Lighting the Other Place. To rise again. To be greeted.

The boat grounded. There were small rocks. One of the men lifted her out. For a moment she did not see, then again she did. They walked towards the sun; he was beginning to drop backwards off the ground, tired out, red with losing. She made the right signs. And they came nearer with every step to the huge things. There was a frightening look, bushes and ferns crushed as it might have been with two bulls fighting, earth scattered, bare stones, strong poles, a tree trunk broken and they came nearer and nearer to the great things. Moon Woman was scared down to her bones. So what had these stones done? The strangers had said that their own Moon Woman was dead. Why, how? The strangers had said she was dead, being stricken with sickness and old. But she herself, was she old? She had children half grown, the boy who had been first to see the strange boat and the two girls, one beginning to look at boys and to be given small things, the other with breasts not full but strong, quick, able to live. Her children, her making. There had been others. She thought of them now and of her man, sad, sad. But I am strong, yes, I can dig, I can carry heavy things. I bleed when the moon tells me. I see well. I see how the moon is looking. But why do they want me? Have their tides stopped? What are these stones doing? She was totally afraid.

They turned away, before coming close to these big stones. But here there was a great house, built of stones and piled turves; it must have taken many seasons to build, a long, long time to go so high. Unless many people worked on it? And the roof poles were very strong, from big trees, and the thatch of heather, tied down strongly, a shelter against anything. She began to stop being afraid. There were more strong poles round the doorway, she could not want to go in but they pushed her through, kindly, laughing a little. She looked round quickly. There were too many people here in the great house, so many she could not know how to greet them. But she was taken by the hand and led into the further, darker part of the house where there was a man painted with sun circles in colours of yellow and red, and with many necklaces and a belt with other colours. Oh he looked big, but he made a good face at Moon Woman. Also he seemed to have a knife of the new stuff. Moon Woman hoped to see and touch it; she had heard stories about such knives.

When he spoke it was not easy for her to understand, though she was becoming used to these strangers' odd ways with words. He was telling her about the great tall stones out there which she had half seen. He said they were so raised to show the way of the sun, who is our master and maker. For the sun moves, watching the world and his people, and sometimes, the wise men say, he becomes shadowed. If this thing happens in a person's lifetime, things must be done to that person, enough at least to make a child cry; this was necessary so as to keep the bad shadow from hurting any person, he or she, and the same must be done to sheep and cattle and goats, even to pigs and certainly to hunting dogs. It had happened in his own father's grandfather's time, but if you knew when it would happen again you could make preparations and instead of every man or woman having to have pain done to them, some other thing might be thought about. Then no harm would come of the shadow and the sun would be whole again and shine on his people. But Moon Woman had not seen this terrible shadow and it was difficult to understand. Yet she remembered the night, just once in her life-time, when her own moon had become shadowed, not gently but quickly and she had been afraid but had done all the needful things with courage and that shadow had passed as quickly as it came. It was the sun's anger, but it did not, in the end, hurt.

Listening to what was said, it seemed somehow that these un-dreamed of stones would tie down the ways of the sun, so that the wise men could warn all the world of the shadowing. And more, these stones could tie down parts of time which could then be used. Both the Great Man with the coloured stripes and circles and also others, among them the yellow man who had taken them into the boat and some older men, spoke of all this to Moon Woman and sometimes she understood and sometimes she was far from understanding, but it appeared that it was necessary also to know when the moon would show herself and exactly where. They said that the moon was the servant of the sun, to do what he wanted, but that, Moon Woman knew, was not right. In her own mind she unsaid it.

All the same Moon Woman was glad that these strangers who called themselves the sun's strong people, had understood that the moon also must be cared for and praised and strengthened. But why had their Moon Woman died, and had her bones been treated rightly? It was hard to ask these questions. Perhaps later she would be told. They asked if she would make the marks to show the moon where to rise. She said yes, but it would not be right to make any marks while the moon was being worn down by the bite that is the sun's jealousy, was perhaps sad, was waiting to go down into the Other Place. Could be hiding. When she comes back, as I know for certain she will do, I shall begin to tell you all you need to know. I am sure of the markings in my own place, she thought, but here I cannot know. Not yet. They said she must go to the great stones. Yes, she said, but not alone. And not yet.

Later there were beautiful torches burning all round the coloured Great Man. They were carried by boys and the smoke smelled of pine resin. She had never seen so much light. But they took her to the women's room where there were little cruisies of shells or rough clay, and her bed place had sweet-smelling leaves and furs of a kind she did not know, very soft and warm. Yes, said one of the women, they came to us in a boat from somewhere else; they are for honoured guests. The room had deep pots of water and on the broad stone shelves there seemed to be many kinds of things, more than she knew. Lying there she heard sweet sounds from the strung sinews of a little harp. She listened to the singing words and thought they were about the moon. Her moon.

In a while she woke and she and the other women ate porridge and cheese and honey and drank creamy milk. But she was tired, dazed, not altogether sure where she was. Again she slept. She woke in a while, stirring when the others stirred. The dawn light was creeping, as it had in her other life. One came in through the woven door curtain, swinging it back and laughing. It seemed she was the newest wife of the Great Man, the one with the colours and the great knife, who had sent his men to fetch her away. He had more wives than one. Perhaps she — but the thought slipped and was gone.

The days of the moon's shadowing passed until one night she was gone and was now perhaps lighting the

Other Place. The Moon Woman was taken to look at the stones, but held back until another woman took her hand. She watched as one stone was put into place. The men had made a slope, there were tree trunks from trees bigger than any she had seen, bigger than trees should be, twisted hide ropes and everywhere so many men. Too many to count. There was heavy singing, as of people doing a big thing together. But she would not go near. Such tangles make one afraid. Then there was shouting and yelling and suddenly the great dead stone was tilted over, was standing, was alive, was pointing at where the sun might be. She was afraid deep inside herself.

How many men? Hand after hand of them. She had seen those she knew, from the old place, yes, they were all there. One had lost a finger when a stone had fallen on it, but it was not his best finger, he could still work and he too was fat. And who feeds them? The sun or the one who stands for the sun in the sun colours, since the sun cannot stay still and appear before us. He must feed them well. They are happy. Yes, he kills fat oxen, sheep, has pots boiling in many, many fires, has porridge, milk, bread and the drink that fizzes in the mouth as the hot stones fizz in water. He has men from everywhere. And it was our own men, she said to herself, who told him about me when their Moon Woman died. They knew that they would be honoured because of me, for I myself am honoured. That was a good thought if it could be kept clear. She kept it beside her, turned it over in her mind.

One day she saw something strange. It was like a cow but it had no horns. Instead its head rose up on a tall, strong neck with dark, shining hair like a young woman's. Also it had a tail of shining hair and it was more decorated with a beautiful collar and dangles than even the best of herd bulls. On its face was a kind of noose, also with dangles and the Sun Man held the end of the noose and the beast blew through his wide nostrils and stamped his feet. She came a little nearer and saw that its feet were not clefted as a cow's feet are, and also it smelled different. Someone told her that this beast had been given to the Sun Man when he went across the water and had his great adventure. If he went there again he would bring back a mate for it. A cow would not do.

This is a very strong beast, the man said. It could pull a big sledge. One of the Sun Man's young sons had got onto its back and held on by the long hair and it had carried him as an ox can carry but faster. Much faster, and the hounds bounced and barked behind it. So, thought Moon Woman, this is another thing which no-one else has seen and when I go back they will not believe me. If I go back. For it began to seem to her that she would not any longer be able to talk easily as in the old days. She had seen so much that was new, seen with her own eyes. Seen and touched.

She cherished the stone that had been given to her and one day the women whispered together and they showed her how one could make a hole in the ear and put a fine sinew through it and then, on that, hang a beautiful stone or a shell or even flowers. Look, they said, and turned her round and round so that she could see. She fingered these dangles and at last she said yes, she too. So they made the holes in her ears and she became more beautifully decorated. Also the skin on her hand was beginning to look smoother and she was quickly becoming strong and fat where a woman wants to be fat, with eating so much and so well. Sometimes she wished she could take a full bowl to her daughters. She dreamed of them but not any longer of her man. The moon came back and Moon Woman tracked her, watching where she moved and how she twisted the stars around. It was good to have her own moon back in this new place. It made her feel easier. She walked a long way some nights, getting stones and bushes into her memory: markers.

She would sleep part of the day, watched over, and then, before moonrise she met and spoke with the wise men, two of whom were old and one younger. They told her about tracking the sun and how to make sure of the seasons. They drew with a stick on a place of smooth sand and she tried to understand, although the words were difficult. You hunt the sun with great stones and he could be tamed, no more doing terrible things, no more allowing the angry shadow. Or perhaps warning of when and why it must come to be? So that preparations could be made, the terror averted? There were suitable presents to be given to the sun. As also to the moon, she thought, and in a while this too was spoken of.

So, they told her, when their Moon Woman died, who was to track the moon and make sure of the tides and the goings-on of the stars?

Fear grew on them. For even the young one, who had been half taught by their Moon Woman, had died with her. How? They had become not themselves, blotched and swollen, crying. A dreadful smell. All those in certain houses had died and the houses had been burnt over them and scattered. Some terrible mistake had been made. That must be so, surely? They had not known what to do. Then one of the men from over there had told them that they too had a Moon Woman. It almost made Moon Woman laugh when they said that she came from over there, somewhere far off, which she knew well meant her own place, her own house, all her certainty. Yet this was how it had seemed to them. Somewhere like in a story.

So she kept quiet and agreed. She could feel that people were anxious, not so much the men and women who were going about their daily work and sleeping sound at the end of it, but the wise ones and those concerned with the sea. Water is always on the move, uncertain, not like the good land. Had their tides changed, even a little? Had the rise not reached a certain rock? It seemed to be worse as the moon waned and, in the end, left the paths of the sky. But all would be well, she said, and the next evening would see the moon come again, a young girl dancing, star-crowned, into the heavens. You are sure of that, they asked, and she said yes. It was something she knew, from inside. She asked for peeled stakes, white, sharpened. This would be necessary for the sight lines. She was not anxious. She knew what to do. It was after this that they brought her two beautiful things, two long pieces of woven colours, such as she had never seen. The other women bathed her and dressed her in these and combed her hair. She became still more certain, more aware of this tie between herself and the moon.

And so it was. For all the days of that moon, while the clear weather had held, as was right, Moon Woman followed the rising and setting. She was no longer afraid of the great sun stones. They knew her and would help her. In the sun's hours she ate and slept and sometimes listened to singing. Mostly she slept in the women's room, but sometimes, if she was too sleepy to find her way she lay out in the grass and heather. Once she woke to see that the wise men and the coloured Great Man were watching her, not too near. She saw that the Great Man was fingering that strange knife he had. It was then that she thought how much honour she was getting here, more than ever in her life before. Did she any longer want to go back? She was frightened to be thinking that, and then all at once it seemed clear. She had left the young one half trained: would she become a true Moon Woman? Yes, she thought, the girl knows the beginnings and everything else follows. If she is in trouble she can come to me here. In a boat, yes, in a boat. I can think of that, but I do not want to go in a boat again. I would like to see my children, but not as much as I like to stay here, to be honoured and looked at. I want to see that strange beast again, to see him run and his long tail shaking. I do not want to go back and talk to old Keeper. But perhaps he is now dead and young Keeper has taken his place.

She shut her eyes again. If I were to say a few small and easy words to the Great Man, if I were to move myself in a certain way, then we would be sun and moon. Then I would put my fingers onto the colour, onto that knife, onto his eyes, ... eyes, onto that round, shining sun that hangs over his heart, fingering it so that my fingers would meet his, me going . . . onto all parts of him. He would be mine as the sun is the moon's.

Should I, then?